MOJAVE
RIFT

MOJAVE RIFT

BOOK 1 *of the* **ARCPOINT SERIES**

J.W. Gilbert

MOJAVE RIFT

Copyright © March 2021 John Gilbert Wozniak

Cover and book design by DesignWise Art

This is a work of fiction. All of the characters, names, and events as well as all places, incidents, organizations, and dialogue in this book are either the products of the writer and illustrator's collaborative imaginations or are used fictitiously.

ISBN 978-1-7344212-1-7

OTHER WORKS BY J.W. GILBERT

Mojave Man
Published by J.W. Gilbert

Mojave Rock
Published by J.W. Gilbert

The Moment
Published by Outskirts Press

Not Your Ordinary Praise and Worship
Published by Elisha Records

Escaping Ignorance - Pursuing Wisdom
Published by Inkwater Press

PRAISE FOR MOJAVE RIFT

"Author J.W. Gilbert did an incredible job of creating a believable background for the story, setting the tone early on and then taking me on a journey alongside Arcon and Elaina. The imagery of the forest and the descriptions of the tribe's life blew me away. It was all so very vivid and picturesque that I had no issue imagining every scene in my head. I could hear Arcon's voice in my head, feel his emotions and enjoy the ride. Mojave Rift is a fast-paced, incredible journey of a lifetime and you shouldn't miss it for anything."
— Rabia Tanveer for Readers' Favorite: ★ ★ ★ ★ ★

"Accessible to all readers due to its moderated content and accessible plotline, this is a thrilling adventure that could be read by young adults and older generations alike. [...] Overall, author J. W. Gilbert triumphs in Mojave Rift, presenting an authentic and well-developed adventure and a promising start to a whole new series."
— K.C. Finn for Readers' Favorite: ★ ★ ★ ★ ★

"Mojave Rift by J.W. Gilbert is an exciting adventure that takes a biblical approach to a post-apocalyptic tale that is endearing, charming, and delightful."
— Liz Konkel for Readers' Favorite: ★ ★ ★ ★ ★

"If there is one thing that gives this novel its strength and depth, it is the handling of character. [...] Mojave Rift is fast-paced, deftly plotted and skillfully written."
— Ruffina Oserio for Readers' Favorite: ★ ★ ★ ★ ★

CHAPTER ONE

MONDAY

"Is this the spot?" Ranger Dan Wilson wrestled with the drone controls to hold its position. Wind gusts were not helping.

Jonathan Greywolf adjusted his wire-rimmed glasses and studied the readouts more closely. "Pull it a little to the west, slowly. When I give the signal, drop it through the clouds."

"Roger that," replied Dan, instinctively searching out the window of the observation tower for the drone. Remembering it was nine kilometers away, he joked, "Jonathan, can I borrow your glasses? I can't see the drone."

Jonathan turned and saw Dan's big, round face smiling at him. He kept the wrinkles on his Native American face unchanged as he replied, "Then we would have the blind leading the lame."

"Touché," said Dan, as he turned to his compass readout for direction.

"Approaching position," said Jonathan. "Now!"

With a smooth movement of the joystick, the stars disappeared from the monitor. "We're in the clouds," said Dan. "Mery, let me know when you have any visuals."

"On it," said his wife, Meredith. She leaned forward, poking her small nose closer to her monitor. "Nothing yet."

"What's the altimeter reading, Jonathan?" asked Dan.

"Twenty-seven hundred feet. Dropping ten per second.

We should be clear by twenty-three. Closing in on twenty-six hundred."

Dan's heart raced as the drone made its descent. He could hear Jonathan's strained voice ticking off the altitude, his wife commenting on the gray in the monitors. But his mind was focused on the mysterious people below the drone. *What had they morphed into during a century and a half of hiding in the Mojave Forest? Had their hearts changed when Jesus returned? Or was this place of theirs still the Devil's Playground?* He hoped to find out soon. "Jonathan, you're the expert on this tribe. Are you sure they're peaceful?"

"I never met them."

"I didn't think you had. I mean, you're only about a hundred years old. But your father did, right?"

"Many times. He said they were good people. But they went into hiding before I was born."

"The last people to see them were met with gunfire," said Mery.

"I wouldn't worry," said Jonathan, it's only a drone."

"Thanks a lot—sure would put me in a tight spot," said Dan.

Meredith sat straight up in her chair. "I'm starting to see definition," she exclaimed. "Oh, Dan, I'm seeing trees." A tear rolled down her cheek. "This is so exciting."

Dan pushed forward on the joystick to stop the drone's descent, then turned to his wife and smiled. "Thanks for being here." He studied the monitor. "Jonathan, I'm holding position. Are we still at the right spot?"

"A little too far west now. There appears to be less wind in the lower atmosphere."

"Roger. That's good news. Are we all ready to take a look around?"

Meredith rested her hand on her husband's shoulder. "Are you excited to see what's in this forest?"

"You have no idea."

Mery clicked her tongue and shook her head. "Dan, you've talked about this mission incessantly for months. You've obsessed about the Mojave People for decades. I have *some* idea you're excited. We could be the first people to see one of them in over a hundred years!"

"Don't get your hopes too high. It's after midnight, so they're probably not out walking around. The main thing is that they don't see us. Central Authority insists that we don't disturb them. That's why we're using this military spy drone," said Dan.

"*Antique* spy drone," said Jonathan.

"Well, with no military for a century, we get what we get. Shall we take a look?" asked Dan.

"Let's go!" said Jonathan. "You're stealth at twenty-three hundred feet. We can expect the props to be heard at twenty-one."

"I'll drop a little so we can see better, and move east. In the middle of the twenty-first century there was an industrial building at the target location. Triangulation placed the source of the code-like radio static in the same area. We should be close," said Dan.

Meredith lurched in her seat. "I thought I just saw some lights."

Dan reversed the drone's direction. "Yeah, you're right." He leaned forward, examining the monitor. "I'm going to head towards them. Watch the thermal imager for a campfire or something. Jonathan, keep tabs on the altimeter. You're right—at twenty-one hundred they'll hear us for sure."

"Got it. You're at twenty-one seventy now, so be careful."

As they moved the drone toward the lights, Dan said, "The archives put the structure around here. Let's hope there's something left of it."

"There it is!" said Meredith, as they flew past a hill.

"Great. I'll start flying a grid pattern around it and record images. We can analyze them later. Try to keep me at twenty-two hundred."

"You're at twenty-one thirty, so go higher," said Jonathan.

Dan pulled back on the stick and Mery yelled, "Dan! The other way! Go up!"

"Oh, yeah, sorry." He pushed the stick forward.

"Okay, that's good," she said in a calmer voice. "Whoa, that's high enough. Don't go up into the clouds."

Dan stopped the ascent and hovered the drone. Then he lurched forward, his chair groaning under his bulk. "Uh-oh. Look."

"There's a person down there," she said.

"I can see that. He seems to be looking up at us. He may see the silhouette of the drone on the moonlit clouds. Oh, now he's running. We may need to cut our surveillance short."

"After all this trouble?" asked Jonathan.

"You're right. These people are under my jurisdiction now. I can't serve them without knowing something about them. This may be our only chance. I'll back off and make a few quick passes over the area to gather information. At least now we have proof the Mojave people still exist."

Dan was silent as he flew the drone in a grid pattern around the area. A beep came from the control panel. "That's not the altimeter, is it?"

"No. It's the battery level," Jonathan groused.

"Okay. We need to hurry. Mery, have you seen anything on the infrared yet?"

Mery shook her head. "I've seen a few spots near the big building, but not much."

"Okay. I'll drop down a little and take another pass."

"Won't they hear the drone?"

"We have to risk it. If you see another spot, holler. I'll try to hover over it."

Meredith kept her eyes focused on the thermal imaging screen as the beeping became more rapid. "Oh, there was one. Go back. That's it. Back, back, back. Right there."

Dan captured the image with the push of a button. "Okay, got it," he said. "That wasn't a very large spot, but it's something."

Mery turned to him. Pushing a strand of her long brown hair away from her face, she asked a question she already knew the answer to, "This isn't what you expected, is it?"

"These Mojave People are elusive, that's for sure. But this is a cold night, so I did expect we'd see some kind of warming fire. We didn't even see fading embers. I really thought we'd find more infrared signatures."

Just then, the battery signal went steady. "Guess that's all we can do. We've got just enough battery power to get back. Going up!"

Dan pushed on the stick and the monitors went dark as the craft reversed through the clouds. When stars appeared, he heard Mery exclaim, "There it is, the tower light!"

"Great. You earned your pay. I'm bringing it home," said Dan.

"You're paying me?" asked Mery.

Dan laughed. "Absolutely … nothing. And you earned every penny."

"I'll invest it on dinner Tuesday night, when Jonathan comes over to help analyze the drone footage," countered Mery.

Jonathan protested. "Wait a minute. Don't I get paid?"

"Same as me," said Dan, with a nod to the affirmative. "Trust me, my wife's cooking is worth it."

Arcon Franklin slipped into his two-room apartment, used a light touch to lock the door, and hurried to undo the leather ties that kept his rabbit skin protective gear secure around his forearms. He tugged them off, stepped out of his moccasins, and darted into his bedroom. Crouching down, he slid a tanned goat hide out from under the bed, bringing several electronic parts with it.

He assembled the pieces into a radio and transmitter on the dining room table as fast as he could and plugged it in. A message from Elaina should be coming through soon, and he didn't dare miss this one. Last night, Raymo the night guard had talked about seeing a spying machine in the sky. *Could the outsiders have located my transmitter?* Luckily no one took Raymo seriously.

Pushing his long blonde hair behind his ears, Arcon donned earphones and listened. He checked the clock, but it'd stopped again. Stretching the cord on the earphones, he leaned to look out his window at the southern courtyard of the Facility. The tree shadows were just striking the upper story, which assured him he wasn't late.

His homemade crystal radio made a faint crackling noise, a hiss, and then went silent. Arcon's heart pumped a little faster beneath his leather tunic, but the static had been a false alarm. He checked the connections.

Most nights he'd pass the time reading a technical manual, but not tonight. This transmission would be Arcon's last contact with Elaina before he left the confines of the community— a place she referred to as The Mojave Forest.

To Arcon his place of home was far more than just a forest. It was the creation, the fortress, and the very lifeblood of the only people he'd ever known. Their official name for this place included the trees, the land, the people, and even the ideals they lived by. This was ArcPoint, and after twenty-two years he was about to turn his back on it, maybe forever.

Elaina. He wondered what she was like. He'd heard her voice once on the radio, but had had no way to respond except by Morse code. At first, her voice had been so garbled, he'd had to ask three times for her to repeat her message. She'd been asking, "Are you one of the Mojave People?" He hadn't known if he was or not, but knew his location had once been called the Mojave Desert. After he'd tapped out the Morse code for [Maybe], the connection had gone silent.

Months later he'd still been scanning to connect with the outside world when there came another transmission, this time in Morse code. It was the same person, and she'd given him her name. Elaina. She'd said it wasn't safe for her to communicate with him—someone might hear. He understood. Communication with the outside world was not permitted.

Five long, high-pitched tones jerked Arcon from his memories—Morse code for the number zero. It was zero hour. He tapped out a response on his spark-gap transmitter—four dots, one dot, dot-dash-dot, and then a final dot—the word [HERE].

He didn't know what the Morse code sounded like on Elaina's side of the Rift. She said others might hear, so they were never on for long. Once a day, two minutes max. That's it. On his end he needed only to lock his door. But even that could draw suspicion. He listened and smiled when Elaina's Morse code came through. [STILL ON FOR DATE?]

Arcon didn't hesitate. He deftly tapped, [ABSO]—short for absolutely. Looking at the cheat sheet in front of him, he quickly added [WANT TO HEAR YOUR VOICE]. He'd written the code for that phrase months ago and now was the right time to use it.

[ME TOO. ANY CHANGE?]

Arcon paused and considered how to keep it short: [NOT ME. YOU?]

[MAY GO EARLY]

He didn't like the thought of her waiting for him to arrive at the rendezvous point. He didn't know what the risks were if she got caught. [WHY?]

[CUZ]

He wasn't about to argue with her. It would eat up time, and over the years he'd learned that Elaina was a strong-willed woman, and he liked that. But, he still hoped to warn her if anything went wrong from his side. He tapped back, [WAIT TWO DAYS].

[FINE].

The report from Raymo the night guard made him nervous. *Do I dare mention the spy machine to Elaina?* He decided not to, just in case the Outsiders were listening. This had to be his last communication with Elaina until they were face-to-face. [LAST COMM TIL RONDAVU. OUT].

No response. He hoped she understood he'd be maintaining radio silence unless something went wrong. Then a flurry of tones came through [Yay. No more static from you. Elaina out].

He smiled and dropped the antique earphones on the table. He wouldn't need them again. *Soon, I'll hear her voice, and watch her lips speak the words. But a lot will have to go right before that happens.* His mind reeled with thoughts about what lay ahead, and what he was leaving behind.

Some day the ArcPoint Community would leave this forest. But, until everyone was prepared to risk it, The Elders said no one should venture beyond the forest's edge. The Elders would decide when the time was right. Arcon was convinced they'd wait until the outsiders invaded the forest. Surrender to an invading force would surely cost fewer lives than the dangers in the land surrounding them.

Arcon was only a day away from facing those unknown dangers, but he had a plan, and he was prepared. He owed it all to his friend and mentor, Jarden. No one knew the land around the forest better than he did. For years Jarden had pointed out the hazards and recommended the best routes.

Their beloved home in the forest was surrounded by a maze of earth cracks that could swallow a person whole. Some were small enough to step over, while others would require a bridge. The worst were hidden under a thin layer of soil and debris that could disappear under your feet. At least three people had to be roped together to survive such an encounter.

Rock outcroppings used to be easy to avoid, but trees and needle-brush hid them now. A person could spend most of a day trying to hack a trail around them. Jarden pointed out the ones he knew about. Arcon's escape route would take him where Jarden had never been. He'd used ancient maps of the area to plot a jagged course that should skirt around the rocks.

The needle-brush was a different threat. It was everywhere. But Jarden was the master at conquering that twisted mass of berry briars and thorny tree rhizomes. Since Arcon's boyhood, Jarden had taught Arcon ways to climb into trees to avoid the thorns. He learned how to walk the branches and jump from tree to tree.

Over the years Jarden had developed a thoroughfare through the trees using ropes to tie distant branches together. His best invention, however, was the rope swing. With rope swings, long distances could be traveled safer in a short amount of time. There were now swingways going four different directions out of the ArcPoint compound. And now there was one more swingway that only Arcon knew the location of—he hoped.

Only the hunters had the skill and upper body strength to handle the swings. Arcon had built his secret swingway to be difficult to find and even harder to use. Hunter Tawny was as tall as Arcon, but he was too young to have the necessary skills. Others had skill, but were too short to reach the branches Arcon had used. All the hunters knew he was building the swingway, but he didn't think they'd found it. They wouldn't suspect he'd built towards the Rift.

For some unexplained reason, the big canyon that everyone called the Rift frightened Jarden. Arcon wasn't considering going that way at first, but Elaina told him if he could get to the Rift, she could get him across. It was the shortest route to the outside world, and was free of earth cracks—according to Jarden. Arcon expected to be at the edge of the Rift within a week.

This journey would be much easier if he could've persuaded any of the hunters to join him. Jarden would've been his first choice, but now he was too old and much too important to the Community. He was considered an Elder, and would certainly try to stop Arcon from leaving.

For over an hour, he tried to discipline his mind to prepare for his exit. Instead, he got sidetracked thinking about those he was leaving behind. He knew a lot of people, but he was close to very few. *Maybe that's just as well. It'll be easier for them to forget me and move on.*

Arcon abruptly stood and unplugged the radio equipment. He reached under his bed and pulled out the other items he'd collected. It was time to get ready.

Roberto Gonzales walked into his home office just as his daughter Elaina was turning off the transmitter. She leaned back in her chair and rubbed her hands together, just like her Mom did when stirring up trouble. His daughter was also smart as a whip, which is why Roberto tended to feel out-gunned, most of the time.

"Well, Dad, I just did what you've always wanted. I've stopped sending Morse code to Arcon—forever," said Elaina with a grin.

Roberto shook his head. He knew she wasn't serious. "You know I've been okay with it for quite a while now."

"Just kidding," she said.

He slid past his own desk so he could face her and sat down on the short file cabinet. "Is your master plan still in place?"

"As long as Arcon can make it happen. If he leaves tomorrow after midnight, he thinks he'll reach the Rift on Saturday, hopefully no later than Sunday. I don't think it'll take that long, so I'm going to get there a lot sooner—Thursday night."

"Thursday? You know you can't do squat till I show up with the Search and Rescue Vehicle. It's got all the ropes and tools. All you can do is sit around and wait."

"I don't mind. It'll give me time to scope out the best route for crossing the Rift."

"Will you use the company drone?"

"Maybe a little. Don't worry. I'll be careful."

Roberto flashed back to helping his daughter up from her first bike crash. Sometimes it was hard to believe she was twenty-one now. "Just remember, even the air space is restricted on the other side of the Rift. Don't be taking the drone over it."

"We'll have to, eventually."

Roberto shook his head. "Girl, I don't know how I let you talk me into this."

"Dad, I know I need to wait for you and the SRV, okay? But if Arcon shows up early, I want to be ready for him. It's easier for me to wait than for him."

"I agree with you there. He won't have shelter, and maybe no food or water. But I still wish we weren't planning to get him across that monster crack in the earth. It's wide, it's deep, and it's unstable. We should've found a safer spot, that's all." He saw the crazed look on Elaina's face. "I know, I know. I'm just being your dad."

"Exactly. But it'll be okay, trust me. Remember, Arcon swings through trees for a living—on ropes. He won't be afraid of heights, and he should be able to climb down into the Rift and back out. It's not the Grand Canyon."

Roberto shifted off the cabinet and ran a hand over his buzz cut hair. "It's not him I'm worried about."

"Oh, come on," she said, getting to her feet as well. "I'm not the one crossing the Rift, he is."

Roberto looked his daughter in the eyes. "I know you, girl. If something happens while he's in that hole, you'll go in after him. That's what I'm worried about." When she lowered her eyes, he knew she was finally listening. "Please promise me, if anything happens, we'll call the authorities, and we'll do it by the book—safely. We won't be concerned about all the trouble we'll face. Understood?"

"I understand, Dad," she said, staring at the floorboards. "I never planned on having to go into that canyon." Elaina crossed her arms and looked at him. "But it was your decision that got us to that location."

"What do you mean?"

"Remember? How many times did you tell me? Central Authority laid down the law about crossing into the Mojave." She drove her point, gesturing this way and that with her hands as she spoke. "It's in the books, it's on the maps, and all the other routes force us to enter into that area. Even contacting him has violated the rules."

Roberto dropped his head and nodded. "I know, you're right."

He felt her lift his chin so their eyes could meet. "Dad, we can do this. I believe God is asking us to. We'll get Arcon across, we'll find out what's going on with him and the Mojave People, and then we'll contact the authorities. We're doing a good thing here—there'll be forgiveness."

Roberto blinked and took a step back. Elaina had her mother's penetrating but welcoming hazel eyes, and her grandpa's broad nose and full lips. Those loved ones were gone, and he couldn't bear the thought of losing Elaina. But she also had her grandpa's passion for helping people, and he couldn't say no to that—any more than he could say no to those eyes. He looked deeply into them and said, "Let's do this."

CHAPTER TWO

Jarden knelt to adjust the height of his office chair for the third time, his compact stature nothing like his lanky predecessor. As the new Chief of Procurement, Jarden didn't plan on being in the chair that much, but he still wanted to be comfortable.

For years the former Chief had kept him running around the Community, asking people what they needed, and what they had to offer. As if it were a military battle, the Chief would make a huge diagram with all that information cross-connected. Then he'd tell Jarden what he should take to whom, and what supplies to get from others.

Jarden had known he could do the same thing in his head. Now that the Chief had retired he could do just that, and save the paper makers a lot of work.

As he set the chair back on its wheels, a knock on his office door alerted him to a visitor. Bill, his old friend and new assistant entered. Holding up one finger, he asked, "Can I have a moment?"

"Bill, how long have we been friends?" Jarden asked.

Bill's mouth fell slack for a moment. He tucked his shirt in better and smoothed a hand across its buttons, managing to appear businesslike, even in moccasins, hemp pants, and a home-sewn shirt. "Gosh, I don't know, over fifty years?"

"Yes, Bill, which means you can always have a moment and you never need to knock." Seeing real concern on Bill's face, Jarden asked, "What's the problem?"

"Well, sir, I've been getting a lot of complaints about Arcon from the other hunters. I thought maybe you'd like to deal with it yourself."

"What complaints?" asked Jarden, fiddling with the chair's position by the desk.

"Well, protocol states that hunters are supposed to travel in pairs for safety reasons. But Arcon often swings off ahead of his partner and then can't be found."

"Arcon can move pretty fast, maybe it can't be helped."

"I know that, but they say it seems intentional. He's also been building his swingway over needle brush so dense even rabbits won't go there. I'm sure you know, that's dangerous and serves no purpose."

"Arcon said he was trying to connect the Sunset and Sowester swingways. It sounds like he's getting into the wash near the Sowester Outpost."

"I suppose that makes sense, but he shouldn't leave his partner. Besides that, he's been pressuring the hemp workers to make him more ropes. Now they're asking me why we need so many." He looked around the room and paused for a moment.

"Was there something else?" asked Jarden, as he sat down in his chair.

Bill hesitated, looking a little thrown off by Jarden's question. "Now, I'm not trying to get the kid in trouble. I like Arcon. But there's something you need to know. He's been telling everyone that you're okay with all this. I need to know from you if that's true. If not, then either I need to come down on him, or you do. If you're fine with him doing what he's doing, then it really isn't fair to everyone else. So which is it?"

Jarden hung his head and rubbed his brow. "Bill, I can't say I know what's going on, but I'll deal with it, I promise. Just give me a day or two."

"Will do. By the way, I saw him heading up the stairs to his apartment about an hour ago."

"Okay. Maybe I'll go talk to him when I'm through here."

Arcon scrutinized his pile of supplies. He'd have to sneak more food out of the kitchen. Fruit from the ArcPoint trees was sparse this time of the year, and not very sweet. Berries from the rhizomes would require protein in order to be consumed, which would mean getting some dried goat or rabbit meat. He'd be gone before the free berries were ripe.

Rabbits. He despised having to kill rabbits. Someone had to do it, or the ArcPoint Community would have serious nutrition issues. Besides, being a hunter was the only job that allowed him to spend every day in the forest, secretly preparing his escape route. He would be on that journey soon, to a place of adventure and freedom. Where he wouldn't have to look a rabbit in the eyes before he took its life. Or, more often than not, set it free.

The goats were someone else's problem. They were rarely slaughtered, because their milk and wool made them more valuable alive. But after living a long, pampered life, they too would serve the Community with needed protein and leather. Arcon always refused that job.

He calculated it would be a six-day journey if there were no setbacks. He had enough food for most of it, and some more was in a cache along the escape route.

His water pouch was good for two days, three if he stretched it. He'd be traveling through unknown terrain, so he couldn't rely on finding a water source. He'd have to take his dew-trap to collect water while he slept.

He thanked God for the recent rains and prayed for dry weather. He didn't want the ropes to be slippery as he made his escape through the trees. *Or do I?* He hated wet ropes, but the other hunters hated them more. It would be difficult for them to follow if it rained. *Father, I leave the weather in your hands, and ask for you to guide my success as you see fit.* Rain would bring a different problem. Wet clothes.

Arcon looked in his closet. He wanted to wear his goat hair pullover so he'd look his best when Elaina first saw him. But he knew it wasn't practical. If it were to rain, he'd need his best gripping gloves, and the softer calf-over moccasins to keep from slipping as he ran down the branches.

Eventually, he'd encounter patches of needle brush with no trees overhead. Hacking a path through that would require the special gloves with the heavy leather on the backs of his fingers. Arcon picked up his discarded arm protectors. He'd need double-layered ones and he'd need to cover his legs. He'd worn chaps in the needle brush while constructing his new swingway. They worked well but were bulky and heavy. If he were being pursued, he'd need to be nimble.

He scrounged around in his closet and found his rabbit leather leggings. When he tried them on, he realized he'd gained a few pounds of muscle since the last time he'd worn them. They were tight, but they'd stretch. He'd just have to be more careful since they wouldn't stop as many thorns as the heavy chaps would.

There was one more thing to check before he packed everything away for the evening. He lifted his goat hide rug off the floor. He'd tanned the short wool hide himself. Not only would it keep him warm at night, the map he had drawn on the leather side would be his guide. He'd make room in his pack for it.

Arcon was about to get out his hunter's pack and load it with supplies when he heard a knock on the door. Someone was trying to turn the knob to open it. Only a few people in the community would do such a thing. Personal privacy was sacred—so respected that no one bothered to lock their doors except for the sake of privacy.

"Who's there?" asked Arcon.

"It's Jarden, son."

The familiar burr of Jarden's low voice was comforting and agitating. Arcon glanced around at the paraphernalia he had lying around. "Uh, okay, just a minute." He stashed the pack and supplies under the bed and threw the goat hide over the radio equipment.

Jarden waited for all of a minute and more. He knocked harder. "C'mon Arcon, open up. I don't care how much mess you have in there."

"Okay, okay." Arcon opened his door a few inches. "What do you need?"

Jarden braced his hands on the door frame. "I need to talk with you, son. I haven't seen you for a while."

"Well, okay, we could go down to…"

"No, right here in your apartment is fine. Can I come in?"

"Well, I…"

"Arcon! It's me. I'm your friend. Now let me in!"

Arcon shrugged his shoulders and motioned him in.

Jarden didn't see much mess in general. "What are you up to, Arcon?" He didn't get an immediate response, and it troubled him. He was used to Arcon speaking freely with him, with both boldness and innocence.

Arcon leaned back, using the dining room wall to prop himself up. "I need to tell you something."

"I figured as much. You've been secretive. What are you up to?"

Arcon walked over to the table, pulled away the goat hide and said, "This."

"What is it?" asked Jarden.

"It's a crystal radio." He laid the goat hide map-side down on the floor and stood on it. "I can listen to the outside world."

"Arcon, you know as a Community we agreed not to concern ourselves with the outsiders. When the time is right, we'll reconnect with them as a united community. Until then we ignore them." Jarden looked around at the other things on the table. "What is this thing?"

"It's a transmitter."

"Meaning?"

"I can talk to them."

"People on the outside?"

"I've been communicating with someone. A girl."

"Hoo boy, that's even worse," said Jarden. "Have you told her about who you are? About this place?"

Arcon pushed his hair back from his face with both hands. "Somehow she figured out on her own where I'm transmitting from. But I can't actually talk with her. This thing just makes a static noise that I turn into letters in code. So I can't tell her much of anything."

Jarden saw the excitement in Arcon's eyes—something he hadn't seen since losing his parent's ten years ago. "I don't know how the Community would feel about this. Most still prefer to keep the outside out."

"Jarden, please don't tell them, I beg you."

Jarden placed a hand on the young man's shoulder, something he'd done time and time again over the years. But, never for anything like this. "Take it easy, son, your secret's safe with me. But how far do you plan to take this? People are getting suspicious."

Arcon opened his mouth to speak, but struggled with what he was about to say. He trusted Jarden more than anyone else in the Community, but was it enough? He searched his heart and found the answer. "I want to go see her."

All the strength in Jarden's solid body seemed to fade. He shook his head slowly. "Leave the Community? Arcon, that's not possible."

"Will they try to stop me? Will you?"

"That's not the point. You've been out there. That forest is impossible to get through. The needle brush in some places is a wall. And like I've told you, eventually the big trees quit and it's nothing but needle brush. You can't walk over it, and you can't get through it. It'll close up as fast as you try to hack a trail through it."

"Jarden, you've told me many times—nothing is impossible. In God all things are possible. I believe the place I'm supposed to be is out there, not in here. I can't explain how I know that. How did you feel the first time you set up a rope and swung to a tree?"

"Painful. I fell," said Jarden.

"Oh. Bad example."

"No, I understand. I felt God calling me to build those swingways. It had been getting difficult to feed the Community, just walking branches. But I can't see you making it out on your own, and I don't think you'll get any help from anyone here. Consider the dangers. And think about the girl on the outside. Can you really trust her? Can you even be sure it's a girl out there and not someone trying to deceive you?"

"Give me a little credit," said Arcon, pacing around to relieve some of his excess energy. "I've gotten to know her over the years."

"Then think about the Community. You could bring bad people down on us and it could destroy us. I think you should let it go. Just see me before doing anything rash."

Arcon stared over at the transmitter. "Okay, whatever you say." He looked Jarden in the eyes and changed the topic. "What brought you here, anyway?"

"I needed to talk to you about complaints I've been getting, about some of the things you're doing, and what you're telling people."

"Complaints from who?"

"Other hunters. You know the rules and why we have them. You're supposed to pair up to go hunting. If you slip off a rope and fall through the needle-brush, it could take hours or days to get out of there. And that's if you're in good enough shape after the fall. Remember what happened to Danner when he landed on his good arm? If Chad hadn't been with him, he'd never have made it out."

"I haven't fallen in a long time."

"Don't just think of yourself. There are complaints that you swing off and leave your partner behind. What if something happened to him? And sometimes you can't be found. Someone could get hurt searching for you. This isn't a game, Arcon. What are you thinking?" Jarden's eyes narrowed. His furrowed brow deepened. "Have you been sneaking off to work on your swingway again?"

Arcon folded his arms and stared back at him. "What makes you think that?"

"The hemp workers are complaining about having to make so many ropes for the hunters. Bill tells me the hunters haven't been asking for them, you have. But that's not what troubles me most. Rumor has it, you've been telling them I'm okay with it. We don't tolerate dishonesty in this community, we can't. I'm starting with you to find out the truth behind this. What's your story?"

"Well, sir, technically you told me I could build my own swingway."

"You agreed to do that on your own time, and with available resources. What it sounds like you're doing is to push the boundaries on both those details."

Arcon hung his head. "I'm sorry, sir. I was excited to finish it—it's going to be great for rabbit hunting. But I promise I won't work on it for a while. I'll give it a break."

Jarden stared at the tall, scrawny young man in front of him, trying to read his body language. His upper body was muscular, but the rest of him needed more meat on the bones. *But is it the rabbit meat he's truly after?* Whatever it was, he could tell this line of questioning made Arcon nervous. "I transferred you to the Sunset Outpost so you could build your swingway, even though it was the most difficult quadrant to hunt in. Tell me again why you wanted to go there, and why you won't let anyone help you."

"It was going to be a surprise. I was trying to connect the Sunset and Sowester Outposts. It would give us an alternate path if the ropes weren't set with either one."

That answer sounded contrived, so Jarden asked, "You didn't think you could go that direction to get out of here, did you?"

"I can't believe you asked me that question," said Arcon, hating this whole conversation. He'd hoped Jarden would leave it alone.

"I have to ask, with what you've said about leaving here. You haven't discussed with me anything about supplies for such a trip. Every direction out of this place you'll run into ground so broken by earthquakes it's impassable without equipment and a crew. The logistics have always exceeded our capabilities. And if you go west, well, that's the worst. You haven't seen the Rift, but I have. You might as well try to climb to the moon."

Arcon grabbed the transmitter, jerked it off the table, and held it out to Jarden. "Here, take it. I won't talk to Elaina anymore. And if it's so important to you and the community, take the radio too. I won't even listen for her."

"Now Arcon, calm down."

Arcon was undeterred. He frowned and edged closer to Jarden with the radio. "No, I mean it. Take it."

Jarden did as he asked, accepting the radio, but then walked it back to the table and left it there. "Maybe you should stay home for a few days and mull things over. Consider all the dangers with such a move. Seek God's wisdom. If you still think you need to leave here, then please come talk to me about it. Maybe we can come up with a plan the community will unite around. Agreed?"

Arcon's grumpy face softened. "Jarden, I agree I could never make it out of here without a plan, and without someone to help me. I'll spend some time to decide if it's important for me to leave at all. The whole idea may not be wise to pursue, so can we keep it between us until I can give it some more thought?"

"We can do that. I'll let Bill know we talked, and that you won't be hunting for a few days. And I'll tell him to inform the hemp workers that they can work on other needs. Let's get together in a few days and talk about this some more, okay?"

Arcon was quiet for a moment. "Maybe I'll come to my senses and we won't have to." Then he smiled at Jarden and winked.

Jarden nodded. "I'll go now, and let you get to thinking. Keep the transmitter. I don't want to have to explain what it is."

"Wait," said Arcon. He grabbed his knife and cut the power cord off the transmitter. "Now you have a reason to trust me," he said, handing the cord to Jarden, "With no questions asked."

Jarden just laughed and took the power cord. "A fair compromise," he said. "See you later, son." He opened the door. "I may want to give your swings a try, when you're done with them."

"Ah, well sir, they may not work too well for you."

"Now, now, Arcon. Remember the physics. My weight may compensate for your height. Don't let this desk flab and gray hair fool you. I can still swing with the best of them."

"Well, I didn't mean, you know…" Arcon stammered. Then he added, "I'd be honored for you to try them, sir."

Jarden smiled and left Arcon's apartment. God was doing something with Arcon, but to what end Jarden wasn't certain, so he silently prayed about it. Arcon called his name, so he turned back around.

"All of this …" said Arcon as he made a sweeping arc with his extended arm.

Then Jarden joined Arcon, pointing to the heavens saying, "From Him."

It wasn't typical for Arcon to do the ArcPoint salute. Jarden hoped Arcon's gesture was an answer to his silent prayer.

CHAPTER THREE

TUESDAY

Arcon's arm ached as he swung at the needle-brush with his machete, trying desperately to get to the nearest tree. He needed to climb higher to get his bearing. He looked around but saw no trees. He must have gotten turned around in this immense briar patch, which seemed to grow denser with each stroke of the machete. Looking back the way he came, no hacked trail remained. Needle-brush surrounded him. He couldn't tell where he'd come from. He started to panic, couldn't breathe—

Arcon almost yelled as he woke from a deep sleep. He was face down in his pillow, one arm twisted beneath him. He rolled over and sat up in bed. His heart raced. He remembered the dream. *Is God trying to warn me of something? Will I soon find myself in such a situation? Should I confiscate one of the community's few compasses, just in case?*

Full consciousness brought no answers, but it eased his fear. The dim light from his window revealed it was too early to get up, but he knew sleep would evade him now. The dream was already fading from memory.

As he got dressed, he thought about what he had and hadn't said to Jarden. He hadn't lied, but his statements had been as misleading as possible. They wouldn't "get together in a few days" because he had a plan. He would leave before daybreak tomorrow.

The trip would be dangerous. If he made it to the other side he'd have nothing, except Elaina. Contrary to what he'd told Jarden, Arcon hardly knew Elaina or anything about her world or how he'd fit into it. He'd put his faith in what he believed God was calling him to do.

It was too early to have breakfast with the others. He could eat alone—which he would prefer—but that could draw unneeded attention. His knotted stomach was begging for some of his grandma's herbal tea and nothing more.

He missed his grandma. If she were still alive, he wouldn't leave without her. Now he was the only Franklin left. Nothing anchored him to the Community.

He knew it could put his convictions at risk, but his heart needed an infusion of family memories before he made his escape. He left his apartment and crept down the stairs toward the Room of Remembrance.

As he entered the room, the smell of musty paper filled his nostrils. He turned on the light. The ventilation fan died long before he was born, so he left the door open to air the room out.

There were shelves of magazines and books and wooden boxes filled with personal papers. Every page was important to somebody or it wouldn't be here.

Behind these shelves was another row filled with battery-operated toys and tools. Jarden said some of these worked when he was a child, but the last battery died when he was a young man. Several car batteries still worked, but one more failed every few years.

Arcon walked past a door marked Ancient Evil. He didn't desire to be reminded of how evil the world outside was before ArcPoint. Whether it still is, he didn't know. ArcPoint had purged all those evil references from the Room of Remembrance when Jarden was young. Arcon was here to find good memories.

He moved to a wall of USGS topographical maps that showed the area surrounding ArcPoint. He and Jarden had drawn the location of the Facility and the routes of the four swingways on them. With his finger, Arcon added what wasn't there—his escape route.

First, he'd fake going to the South Swingway, then sneak to the Sowester. Before reaching the end of that swingway, he'd hop over to his own, which headed toward the Sunset Outpost. The hunters knew he was working on this section of swingway, but not how to get to it.

He'd started building it at the Sunset Outpost, but no one had the nerve to jump to the branch they needed to access it. It ended near the Sowester Outpost, but only Arcon knew where. Every so often there would be a gap in the swings, so you had to run branches to reach the next one. And somewhere in the middle, where no one could find it, was another swingway that ventured into uncharted territory.

Jarden had drawn a line in crayon from the Cady Mountains around to another hill west of the Sunset Outpost. He called it Far Ridge. Hunters were not supposed to cross that line. The trees were sparse, the needle-brush was thick, and the rocks were treacherous. No one would suspect Arcon of being in the midst of it all.

Arcon stared at one spot on the map. It was visible from the often-manned Sunset Outpost. This is where his secret swingway ended, and all the unknowns began. If he could make it through the ravine without being seen, they'd never find him.

From that point he'd be in the Wilhelm Wash, which led to the tree-covered Mojave River. Crossing that wet area would put him at an auto-path everyone called the I-15. If he could find it, he'd follow it to Elaina. It was a good plan, and thankfully, not one Jarden had ever seen.

He left the maps and moved to a table marked Transportation. There were models of trains and planes, and a lot of toy cars and motorcycles. On the wall above were pictures of ArcPoint people standing next to some prized vehicle. Both of them were long gone, except for the repurposed car parts. The owners were all in the cemetery, along with his parents.

He picked up one of his favorite books titled Unique Autos of the 20th Century. He longed to travel as they had. Driving, flying, even riding a bicycle would be better than always walking. At least he was one of a lucky few that could swing.

He was admiring a picture of a DeLorean, when he heard footsteps behind him. A woman's voice said, "Well, you're up kinda early."

He turned and saw Madelyn McCoy, leader of the hemp workers. "Hey, Maddy. Sorry about working you guys so hard."

"That's okay. I saw Jarden, and he told me we could do something else if we needed to. He put your project on hold for a while."

Arcon cringed inwardly. "Jarden told you what I was doing?"

"We all knew you were building a new swingway. He just said you were getting overzealous to finish it, that's all."

"Yeah, you know how it is." Arcon grinned and said, "Jarden thought I might be getting jungle fever so he restricted me to the Facility. What brings you to this place?"

"Knotting whatsoever," she joked. "Since I don't have to work on your ropes, I'm checking out some knotting techniques. My grandma put our best book about macramé in here somewhere. I need to fix my chair."

"Sounds like something I should read. I know how to tie a rope to a branch or a goat and that's about it."

She laughed as she walked to an area labeled Crafts. "Well, we all have our specialties. I'd never be able to fix a disc player."

Arcon hung his head. "It worked for a couple movies."

"The point is, you're the only one who's been able to fix one for, well, all of *my* life. It may not have lasted, but everyone loved it." Then she held up a well-worn picture book. "Aha, here it is." As she walked toward the door, she added, "See you at breakfast."

The walls were a mess of photos and papers competing for space, except for one dedicated to the founding days of ArcPoint. Pushed against it was a memorial set up for the ten Founders.

In the forefront was Dr. Norman Ashford, the most important man to the survival of the ArcPoint Community. As a botanist he developed the desert-tolerant ArcPoint tree, which produced a biodiesel fuel for the stoves, generators, heaters, and even the blowtorches the metal shop used. He'd also been instrumental in developing sustainable crop varieties.

Behind his memorial was a row dedicated to the six men and two women who'd put up the lease money for the property that had become ArcPoint. They'd been the de facto leaders of the community for most of their lives. Nearly all of them had been scientist friends of Dr. Ashford or construction coworkers of Lee Franklin.

Arcon looked to the top row, where a lone picture stood. His great-great-grandfather, Lee Franklin, the one with the vision and call of God to develop this place. Propped to the left was the original drawing of the ArcPoint compound and the building he was in, which was simply called The Facility.

To the right was what Arcon had come for—his Grandpa Lee's journal. Many in the community had copies, but no one was allowed to remove the original from the Room of Remembrance except Arcon. As the sole heir, it belonged to him, but he'd never read it himself. As a child, his grandma read to him nearly every day from either the Bible or this journal.

Arcon didn't have the time or the paper to transcribe his own copy, so he lifted it from its stand. Jarden had given him time to reflect, and this is where he'd begin.

Roberto checked the weather report. Elaina yelled from the other end of the house. "Dad, I confirmed our reservation at the Rift Carlton in Calico, starting Thursday night." Roberto pushed himself up and headed in her direction. She yelled again, "They said I could reserve it no charge for up to a week."

Roberto walked into her room. "That place is expensive. We'd better not stay that long."

Elaina turned away from the monitor and looked at him. "I know, but it's the only cabin with a view of that part of the Rift. We can set the telescope up and not have to move it. That's worth a lot."

"You're right, there," he said. "Outside we'd have to explain what we're looking for. People rarely train a high-powered telescope on a forest and a cliff for days at a time."

"Good point." She spun around and clacked away at the keyboard. He watched her kinky, raven-black hair sway. Before it could settle, she whirled again. "Do you think he'll be able to send Morse code with smoke signals?"

"Any smoke will do. All we need is a sign. Smoke will attract less attention than a guy standing on the old freeway, waving his arms. Plus, it'd be easier to pinpoint with the telescope."

"That's true." Elaina turned back to her monitor. "We don't need extra spotters do we?"

"Why do you ask?"

"Well, those friends of mine—the ones praying for us to be successful—they want to know if they could come up to Calico. You know, in case we need help."

Roberto thought about that. "We can't keep them from going to Calico. But we're the professionals. As Search and Rescue, we'll just happen to be in the right place at the right time with the right equipment to help someone. Better if they stay home. Tell them we'll keep them informed so they can pray for us with understanding."

"I agree," she said, tapping away at her keyboard again. "I think they're excited. It's taken a lot of years." She took a closer look at what she'd written, made a couple changes, and hit *send*. "I find it interesting that none of us are getting a check in our spirit that something's wrong."

"Yeah. To hear rumors about the Mojave People you'd think we're about to open the cage to some form of evil.

You understand at some point we must turn that judgment over to the authorities."

"I know, I know. But please, can we spend a few days getting to know him before we do that? I want a chance to talk to him with something other than funny hissing noises." Elaina looked at her dad and they both started laughing.

Roberto shook his head. "Girl, I'm still so impressed you saw a pattern in that annoying static at fourteen."

"You probably would've just changed channels."

"Or thought I needed to get the scanner fixed. Well, it's been a long journey, but we're almost home."

"It's Arcon who'll need a home."

"One thing at a time, girl." Roberto Gonzales stared out the window and said under his breath, "One thing at a time."

CHAPTER FOUR

Thanks to a burned-out wick in his oil lamp, Arcon had to sit by the window to get enough light to read the journal. He recalled many parts, but wanted to remember it all more clearly. His grandma never read it front to back, so he decided to open to the first page:

> *I'm writing in this journal only because someone told me it's a good thing to do. He said I should be honest, so, there you go. He said this isn't a diary, so doing it every day isn't necessary. Good. I don't have time for that. I'm supposed to record things I see God doing in my life. Answers to prayer. Insight from the Holy Spirit. Things like that. There's no need to date it because these things should be timeless, eternal, forever.*
>
> *To start with, I'll do some catch-up. Three months ago, Victoria caught me with a gun to my head. Instead of freaking out, she just told me if I wanted to meet Jesus, I should do it without a bullet. I always thought her belief in God was silly, but it gave her a peace that was overpowering at that moment. She let me have it. The peace, that is. A week later, I realized something. The urge was gone that often pushed me to end it all. Fought that thing for years, but not at all since that day.*
>
> *I still don't know if I would have faced eternal torment after the bullet, or nothing at all. What I do know is,*

I would have missed the joy I have now. With God, with her, and with life itself.

I have to admit I'm frustrated. I can't seem to find very many people as excited about God as I am. I want to share how God has changed my life and changed me as well, but most folks sort of zone out when I bring it up. Maybe that's what this journal is for. We'll see. Or should I say, I'll see.

Arcon closed the journal. His grandma must've never read the first pages to him at all. Maybe because she didn't want him to know Grandpa Lee had considered killing himself. Suicide was one of the ancient evils the ArcPoint community had purged from its midst. It hadn't been done, or even considered, so far as he knew.

Arcon's belly grumbled. He wanted to keep reading but was also curious to see who, besides Madelyn, would show up in the dining area. Talking with others at breakfast was rare for him and might draw suspicion. This wasn't a normal day, but it had to appear like one. He looked in the mirror and mussed his long blond hair, twisting in a few knots for good measure.

Halfway out the door, a memory flashed. Grandpa Lee used to share his faith, in fact he was known for it. Grandma had said he was a street preacher. Arcon wondered when that happened and went back to the journal. He scanned the text.

Met a street preacher today. I always hated hearing those guys when I'd go downtown. Now I have a different perspective on their message, and I think I understand their need to share it. I don't think this guy was accustomed to someone wanting to listen. When he stepped off his soapbox, I asked why he did it. He said God called him to do it. It didn't matter to him if people objected. He left it to God to make them understand. I'll have to think about that. Maybe try it some day.

Arcon skipped ahead, looking for something about him preaching. A few pages farther he found:

I'm not sure how these guys do it. Preaching at strangers is like talking to the wind. Most won't make eye contact. Some cross the street to avoid me. A few listen for a while, then move on. I don't know if I'm having an impact or just wasting my time. I'm not sure if I'm called to do this. It's frustrating.

Arcon scanned to the next page and found this entry:

Lost it today. Some jerk started yelling about God being in everything, and he didn't like me shoving my religion down his throat. Guess he didn't know I hate religion. I asked him what he thought about Jesus. When he said Jesus was a great teacher, I asked him if Jesus was Lord of his life. He hedged that issue repeatedly and then suddenly yelled, Jesus is NOT Lord. That struck a nerve. I pointed that out with a finger on his chest. He shoved me. I shoved back. When the cops showed up, they arrested me!

I need to search myself and rethink if God has truly called me to street preach. And I need to be more diligent about writing in this journal. Then maybe I'd know how I got to this low point.

Arcon looked back and forth through the previous pages. A length of time must be missing. He'd been told Grandpa Lee gave up street preaching to work on the ArcPoint plan. But he hadn't seen anything about ArcPoint yet.

His search was overridden by a growling stomach. He closed the journal and headed for the dining hall.

"Mornin' Arcon," said Chad, Arcon's current hunting partner. They both walked into the kitchen. "I hear you're not going out today."

"News travels fast," said Arcon.

"News doesn't have far to travel, unless it's out there," said Chad, motioning towards the forest.

"Sorry, I was gonna tell you myself so you could get another partner if you wanted."

Chad waved him off. "Ahh, it's just as well. They say it'll rain this afternoon. You know I don't like slippery ropes."

Arcon laughed. "I know, but after a while you'll just grip harder when you see that shine."

"Yeah, yeah. How old were you when you first discovered you *hadn't* gripped hard enough? Good thing Jarden tied training knots for us newbies."

"I didn't use those childish things."

"Oh, the truth comes out. I'll bet you practiced on your own, too. Who had to come rescue you from the needle-brush?"

"No one," said Arcon in mock annoyance. "I crawled out on my own with just a bad rope burn and a few scratches."

Chad laughed once. "That's why you're better than the rest. You've learned from your mistakes because you've made a lot more of them."

"Can't argue with that."

"Hey, when you finish the new swingway, who you gonna have swing with you?"

"Oh, probably Tawny," said Arcon. "No offense, but I designed it to work best with us lanky ones. In fact, he may pass me up one of these days."

"Are we talking height or speed?"

Arcon grunted. "Height. I'll be as old as Jarden before Tawny can swing faster than me."

"I'll tell Jarden you said that."

Arcon picked up a tray and perused the breakfast buffet selections. "Speaking of which, I heard you've told Jarden other things, like that I've been leaving you alone in the forest."

"That's not what I said," said Chad. "Bill found me on my own and asked where you were. Had to be honest so I told him I didn't know. He figured the rest out himself."

"I'm just needling you," said Arcon, as he heaped more omelet onto his plate. "Sorry. I got distracted with the new swingway that day and wasn't thinking."

He waited for Chad to finish dishing up and they walked into the dining hall. Arcon saw Madelyn reading at a table. After an exchange of glances, she went back to her book, and they sat at another table. Arcon was glad she was busy, and hoped to get away from Chad soon. He wanted to get back to his room before too many showed up for breakfast. Especially Jarden.

Ranger Dan shook hands with his friend. "Mr. Greywolf, welcome to our humble abode. You remember my wife?"

"I don't know, it's been a long time."

"Almost two days," said Meredith.

"It seems like just yesterday. Good to see you again, Merideth. I'm excited to sample your cooking. Dan sure seems to like it."

"I do my best. You can call me Mery ..." she said, directing a nod towards her husband. "He does."

"I noticed that. Call me Jonathan," he said, giving Dan a glancing look.

"All right, it's settled then," said Dan. "I'll call you Jonathan, and in a little while she'll call you for dinner. Now, come over and see what we recorded in the Mojave."

They moved into the living room. Jonathan could see a dark monitor with a few blurred light patches on its screen. "What do you have?"

"This is from one of the hi-res cameras." Dan pressed the remote, backing up a few frames before pressing play. "What does that look like to you?"

Jonathan squinted at the monitor. "How far away was the drone?"

"As near as I can calculate, about a hundred meters," said Dan.

"I thought you said it was high resolution."

"It was, a hundred and thirty years ago. I think I was moving too fast."

"Can you run that again?"

"Sure." They watched, as the square blob of light slowly grew larger, then suddenly disappeared, except for a faint glow.

"Based on its shape, my guess is we're looking into the window of a building. It gets brighter as we approach, and disappears as we go over the roof, except for a faint glow on the ground."

"That's what Mery and I think. Exciting isn't it? To think there are humans living in homes with man-made lighting, and not just huddled around a campfire?"

"I wouldn't exactly call it exciting, but it is pleasing to know they are as I expected them to be."

"I didn't know what to think," said Dan. "But this is what I hoped for. I don't want anyone in my jurisdiction living a hard life. Now let me show you what has me confused." Dan closed that file. "Wait a minute." He opened one titled *Thermal Set 4*. "Let me show you this one first." As the picture started playing, he asked, "Is that an animal or a human?"

Jonathan watched the small yellow blob for a while before committing. "I believe that's a human. From overhead, animals would be long and narrow. That object is short and wide, and you can see the limbs moving. Animals would have their legs under them. This creature is walking upright. I say it's human."

"Again, we agree. Now, take a look at this." Dan loaded *Thermal Set 7*.

The monitor stayed dark until a bright ball of white and red moved through. "Once more, please," said Jonathan. "Slowly. Try to stop it directly over that spot."

Dan backed up, hit pause, and then went frame by frame until he was directly over the area. "Intense, isn't it? This is the spot Mery saw."

"Judging by the colors, it's a very hot spot. Since it's round, it has to be a chimney of some sort." He was quiet for a moment and then asked, "Can you find this with the hi-res footage?"

Dan scratched his head. "I don't remember seeing it, but I could sync it with the timestamp. What are you thinking?"

"Just a theory. I'll tell you after you find that spot."

"Okay," said Dan. He fussed with the files on his computer and searched through various images. "It should be in this area."

"Go slow," said Jonathan. He watched as Dan went frame-by-frame through nothing but darkness. "Wait, what was that?"

"I saw it too," said Dan. He reversed one frame and a dull red glow appeared on the screen. "This must be the hot spot.'

They both stared at the anomaly. "Look at the left side of the screen," said Jonathan. "Oh, and on the right as well. See that dull glow? That's the same thing we saw when we looked at the glow from the window. Those could be lights shining out of a building. If that chimney were part of a fireplace, the heat would drive people out of that small building. I believe that's the chimney of a generator. A big one."

Dan's eyes got as big as saucers. "You really think so?"

"Don't know for sure, but what else could it be?"

Dan eyed Jonathan. "If they have electricity, then they aren't primitive."

"And you shouldn't have to worry about them lacking resources," said Jonathan. "Does this knowledge give you the peace you were seeking?"

Ranger Dan hung his head, and with a quivering voice said, "Yes. Yes it does. I probably should have had more faith in God to care for these people. It seems he has."

"Like my dad, I believe our Lord protected these ArcPoint people."

"I shouldn't have doubted you about that. I'm sorry to have bothered you."

"No bother at all. There is more joy in my heart now than when I knocked on your door. And I think Jesus is glad that you know, and that you care about them."

CHAPTER FIVE

Arcon closed the door to his apartment, crossed to the window, and stared out at the ArcPoint forest. From this second-story vantage point he could see the path he'd take to flee this place. People crisscrossed it below.

He looked to his right and, although he could see only trees, in his mind he pictured Elaina. She lived somewhere towards the southwest in a place called Apple Valley. He'd crafted many plans to walk around the south end of the Rift to get to her. It looked so simple on the USGS maps. But they didn't show the earth cracks or the rocks. Jarden called it deadly to try alone. At least with the Rift route he had some help.

On most days he didn't appreciate the attention he received from being the sole survivor of the great Founder, Lee Franklin. But it had its benefits, and this apartment was one of them. This sprawling Quonset hut style Facility acted like a huge Faraday cage. All of the metal in the roof and the walls blocked outsiders from hearing radio signals. Only on the ends could a signal get sent out. And only this apartment had a direct path in the direction of Elaina.

Turning towards the south, he focused on his plan. He spent months surveying the rarely traveled trail, walking great distances along it with his eyes closed. The only way to gain an advantage over pursuers would be to travel in the dark of night, and to lead them in the wrong direction.

Not long after first light, they'd notice he was gone. Someone, probably Jarden or Bill, would call in the hunters, the ones who could recognize Arcon's long footprints. It was their responsibility to find one of their own who'd lost his way.

Arcon stroked his scruffy beard and scrutinized every step of his plan. He shook his head as if to dislodge the thoughts. *Too late to change anything with the plan. I need to focus on Elaina.* And it was too late to change anything with her as well, so he just stared out at the forest.

According to Jarden, these particular Acacia trees grew nowhere else on earth. They were never supposed to grow anywhere, period. Geneticists worked for years to create a tree that was disease, drought, and salt tolerant. They were engineering a rootstock to graft other plant varieties onto. The Acacia Root Construct plant was never designed to have a life of its own.

Early on, the trees went wild, then took over. The Community wasn't concerned at first because the trees were beautiful and held many health benefits. Because they were so hardy, they grafted many varieties of nuts and fruits onto them. If not for this rootstock, the ArcPoint Community would not have survived through the desert years.

Arcon was thankful they were genetically engineered to be thornless; otherwise travel across them would be impossible. But from their trunks grew rhizomes with wicked thorns. He'd lost a lot of blood on them. Without someone to prune them, they would blanket the ground around every tree.

Nearly a hundred and fifty years ago, Dr. Norm Ashford planted thousands of these experimental plants in the Mojave Desert soil. He grafted various oil producing plant buds onto this rootstock while working for the Renewable Energy Development Consortium. He hoped to find a biodiesel fuel source that didn't require the destruction of rain forests. He had limited success with the grafted trees, but the wild rootstock thrived.

The geneticists referred to this rootstock as ARC 5.0, since it was the fifth attempt at producing a viable Acacia Root Construct plant. Years later, when the thorns showed up, the Community dropped the five and zero and the name ArcPoint was formed.

The trees Arcon saw out his window were all wild. He wondered what Dr. Norm would think about the effort poured in to domesticate them. He considered them the most invasive species on earth.

Something must have gone wrong with the gene splicing. Even Dr. Norm didn't understand why the rhizomes had thorns. Or why they grew berries. Or why the seeds from those berries produced a delicious blackberry, also with thorns.

It didn't help that ground squirrels were quick to bury tree seeds everywhere. Once the rains came, the landscape became peppered with new trees, rhizomes, and blackberry vines. ArcPoint people called the whole twisted thorny mess *needle-brush*.

For all the bad, there were some positives. The fruit was tasty when it was ripe. When dried, the tree seeds could be ground into flour. Oil from those seeds ran the generator. A chemical in the bark would tan leather.

Arcon wouldn't miss the thorns, but wondered if he would ever see the beautiful Acacia flowers again. Would he smell their fragrance, or enjoy the delicate butterflies that danced on them? Would he run along the branches, or eat the tasty fruit? *Will I ever return to ArcPoint?*

He wondered how the idea of forming this community had first occurred to Grandpa Lee. Back at his desk, he scanned the journal for the term *ArcPoint*. The first mention of the term ARC was near the beginning. It was also the first mention of Dr. Norman Ashford.

Knocked Norm off the fence today. Hadn't talked to him since the breakup of the Consortium. We had a fascinating discussion about genetics, DNA, plant genomes, and more.

He was excited to tell me how successful those new Acacia trees are, what he called ARC plants. He described all the genetic modifications done to create them, how desert and disease tolerant they had become, how much biofuel they could produce, and how several varieties of plants could be grafted onto the rootstock. Impressive!

Now I know why I was given so much money to build the Facility. If the operation hadn't been shut down, this tree would have changed the future of mankind, and made us wealthy along the way. He agonized over having to abandon them in the desert.

I never knew plants had genes like humans do. Norm says DNA contains all the computer-like programming for making any living organism. Even a skin cell on my elbow is there because DNA says it's supposed to be.

I had to ask: If DNA is like computer code, who wrote it? He said science didn't know, but they're working on it.

Up to this point, all I cared about DNA was that because of some flaw in that code, cancer cells could grow out of control and kill my sister. If science knew how DNA evolved, why didn't they know how to correct cancer-causing defects?

I told Norm I believed God created both the DNA and the organisms. He said he didn't believe in an all-powerful creator. I said I thought DNA popping into existence before organisms took more faith than I could imagine.

I gave him my God analogy using the construction of the Facility. Plans had to happen first, so every part of the facility got built right. Once built, over time the building falls apart. God's perfect creation, the DNA, is falling apart with the passage of time. He said my logic matched the facts. I didn't expect that.

Norm said he was confused because he knew I was an atheist. I told him about my suicide attempt and he gave me a big hug. I think it shocked him. I shared how God changed me from the inside out. He said he could tell I was different, but couldn't put a finger on why.

I told him not to worry about rejecting religion. I still do. But God is real, and I can't reject that. He shouldn't either. God created the incredible beauty in nature to amaze us humans, but bees aren't impressed by the color of flowers.

Anyway, we talked about that for over an hour. Then he said he wanted to know more about creation. I pointed to the sky and said, "Give your life to him and let him show you." He did it, and it seemed genuine on his part. We'll see if it sticks. Hope so. I like the guy. I could use a believing friend. Besides Victoria, of course.

Arcon's grandma never talked about what went on before the ArcPoint community. Dr. Norm developed the trees and Grandpa Lee built the buildings, but Arcon didn't know they'd been unbelievers at the start. Others must, because copies of the journal were floating around. *Maybe it doesn't matter.*

Arcon knew he hadn't yet read the entire story, what his grandma called the biggest miracle of them all. It involved the start of the ArcPoint Community Endeavor. He read another entry:

What a strange night. I had called together every believer I knew to pray for the many people that have suffered this past week. The Mitchells lost two family members at a mass shooting. Nine friends were injured at a so-called peaceful protest. Three house break-ins. A wildfire destroyed the Brady's home.

I was suffering too, on the inside. The church we attend no longer allows personal testimony. We used to hear of healings or prophecies, but that's been halted. Meanwhile, government seems more corrupt and scandalous every day. Believers are turning to metaphysical stuff right and left. I thought believers would never see tribulation, but we may be in it already.

While our group was praying for those with troubles, a thought suddenly came to me. I don't know if it was a vision, but I pictured my dad throwing a big barbeque in our backyard. A shoving match started between two men.

Somehow my siblings and I were young. Dad told us to go to our rooms. He needed to take care of something and didn't want us to watch. What I saw was so real. I shared what I saw with everyone, but I didn't understand it.

Later, Norm told us he'd just come from the Mojave. He'd needed to get away to some place peaceful and ended up visiting our old workplace. Since it was supposed to be abandoned, he was surprised to see some property owners there. They said they'd thought about hiring us both to oversee moth-balling the buildings. I'd hate to do that, but I could use the work.

Someone else told us he'd been reading in Acts where all the believers laid everything at the Apostles' feet and had all things common between them. They didn't give it to the poor; they shared it with those among them who had need. They did it to survive the persecution that was coming on the believers in Jerusalem. We discussed it briefly, then returned to praying.

At one a.m. I awoke and my head was filled with wild ideas. If the Consortium was abandoning the facility, what if some of us moved out there? Norm could play with his trees, and we would be away from the anarchy of the big city.

Can't wait to run it by Norm. Victoria thinks I'm crazy, but she's not opposed to it. I can think of others who may be interested. But they have to be believers, not only in God, but also with this wild idea.

Arcon knew the rest. The dad in Grandpa Lee's vision was God, the brothers were the ArcPoint people, and the room they went to was the Mojave. His grandma often quoted the Bible verse that confirmed the vision, *Go home, my people, and lock your doors! Hide yourselves for a little while until the Lord's wrath has passed. Isaiah.*

The Founders wouldn't accept possessions like they did in the book of Acts, but everyone did give freely to build up the Community. And someday the Father will open the Mojave door and say it's time for his children to come out. The trouble is over; he ended the fight.

For over a hundred years, no one has attempted to sneak out for themselves to see if it's safe to leave. All this time they've been content. Not Arcon. Tonight he'd see what's out there.

CHAPTER SIX

Noreena Chan grabbed the doorknob, twisted it slightly, then pulled away. She was embarrassed by the fear she felt, and by the snickers of those next in line. *I can do this. I have to.* She grabbed the knob once more and opened the door. She almost fainted at the sight. There was no ground in view for thirty meters in front of her or below her. She stepped out and gripped the handrail as vertigo made her feel like she was falling. With one hand, she closed the door behind her. She moved a few feet down the wraparound porch, staying snug against the old building. Then she smiled. *At least I didn't scream like the next person just did.*

She scurried past the end of the building and away from the edge of the Rift. She looked back at the house-turned-tourist attraction she'd just been in. Someone in the past had opened that same door with no safety railings or walkway. The Rift was only two meters wide then, but was not the correct path of retreat during an earthquake. She shivered just thinking about what that experience must have been like.

The next attraction was a transparent walkway protruding over the canyon. At this point she'd had enough adrenalin for one day. But she'd already paid for it, and if she didn't finish this next challenge, her colleagues would say she failed.

Traditional seismology reports said California was overdue for another big one. Noreena, however, put her hope in the promise of a Sabbath rest, that for a thousand years planet earth would be free of the shaking devastation it experienced in the mid 21st century. Family superstition held, if another earthquake did ever hit, she'd be right in the middle of it.

She rejected that fear, and took a step of faith over the edge. At the end of the walkway she gripped the rail and looked up and down the Rift. *Here is where it started.* What began as a small earth crack here in Fort Irwin would eventually spread from Twenty-nine Palms in the south to Reno in the north. Three Interstate freeways became impassable. Over a century later, only I-80 has been rebuilt.

As she walked back toward solid ground, she focused on the town in front of her. Fort Irwin was a military training center when the first major earthquake hit. When an earth crack cut off access to the airstrip, they migrated the base and its supporting town to other locations.

Once the turbulent geology settled down, Fort Irwin became the perfect location to house thousands of annual visitors to the area. The Training Center had many mock villages that became dwelling units for overnight guests.

Noreena saw the Rift as symbolic of the many ways mankind was once divided. When Jesus returned, he healed the rifts between nations, races, genders, and religions. But He left the scar of the CalNeva Rift as a reminder.

Arcon meandered past the dozens of tiny houses situated north of the Facility. He'd just read in the journal about the controversial birth of this 'illegal subdivision'. The government had demanded the removal of these non-recreational dwellings. After the I-15 freeway broke in half, the government stopped bothering them about it. The only access for San Bernardino governing forces was through Arizona, then Nevada, and back to the Mojave. The County had bigger crime issues than building code non-compliance.

In the journal, his grandpa regretted purchasing the homes. Now residents hail Lee Franklin as a visionary. It took decades for ArcPoint trees to grow large enough to provide material for log homes. Those years would not have been bearable with over three hundred people crammed into the Facility or camping outside it.

Photos of the subdivision houses hung in the Room of Remembrance. At that time each had its own unique color scheme. Now they're all covered in the same coat of dirty blue. In a few years they will make a new batch of paint. Every person in the Community will descend on these houses to paint them. With no way to store the paint, it will all be used up the same day it's made. Arcon will regret missing out on the fun.

They eventually designated the tiny homes as newlywed cabins. Scattered through the forest are large log cabins for families with children along with the older generations. Single young men live in Facility apartments.

Individual choice gave way to survival. But Arcon always wanted to build his own home, for his own family, in a place with a view beyond the trees.

He stopped at house number twenty, where Grandpa Lee first lived with Grandma Victoria. It's been empty since his parents moved out when he was born. Designated the Franklin Home, it's reserved for him to take a wife and move into. But Arcon was never inclined to live there.

Arcon turned at the sound of a door opening behind him. A pretty blonde girl was emerging from cabin nineteen—the very girl the Community expected him to take as a life partner.

Brina descended from Dr. Norman Ashford. She was considered a miracle child, and being born female was more rare than being born to a couple in their seventies, as Arcon was. But both of them were born into the families of the two greatest Founders? That was clearly seen as a God thing, by everyone but Arcon and Brina.

"Hi, Brina," he said as their eyes met. "Visiting Lori?"

"Yeah. I took her another start of Grandpa's African violets. Hers keep dying."

"Well, no one could grow things like your Grandpa Norm. Didn't he leave notes on how to care for them?"

"I gave her the notes, but I think she over waters them. I've got lots of starts though. What brings you out here?"

That was not a question Arcon could answer with a straight face, so he looked around, scratched his head, and said, "Gee, I don't really know."

Brina laughed. "Well, if you don't know, then you can walk me back to the dye house. I have a couple vats of yarn to pull."

"I'd be glad to," he said, offering her his elbow. He was glad the two of them had cleared the air about their relationship. They had enjoyed playing together as children, but the forced matchmaking of the Community had split them apart. Now they were again comfortable with just being friends.

As they walked arm in arm, Brina asked, "Aren't you afraid people will talk?"

"Let them." He wished he could tell her about his plans, and about the other girl in his life. She would understand and wish him the best. She may not forgive him for failing to say goodbye.

The view from the Rift's Ranger Station Tower was awe-inspiring. This Rift had to have been a phenomenal earth-shaking event. From this elevated position, Noreena could see almost a hundred kilometers of broken earth. With the tourist telescope, she found the town of Fort Irwin. To the south was a waterfall.

"Find what you're looking for?" asked a booming voice behind her.

Startled, Noreena turned to see a very large man in a ranger's uniform, sporting an even larger grin. She stammered out, "I wasn't looking for it, but I see a waterfall down there."

"There are two, actually—one on top of the other. The lower one spills out of the rock about ten meters down and runs most of the time. The one that spills over the rim only runs for a few days after a rain and hides the other one. If you take the trail, you can look back and see both."

"I must check that out while I'm here."

"The top one will be gone soon, maybe tomorrow. Unless it rains. Are you here for a few days?"

Looking at his name badge, she replied, "Until Thursday at least, Ranger... Dan."

"And your name is?"

"I'm Noreena Chan. I'm a reporter with ..."

"The San Bernardino Portal, right?"

"Have you read my articles?"

"To be honest, I scan everything and read very little of it. But your online news serves my area, so I appreciate you folks keeping me informed of things."

"Your area?"

"Yeah. I'm the authority over San Bernardino County—the land, not the people or cities. But I like your articles. You do the human interest stuff, right?"

"Correct—the people, not the land or the cities."

Laughing like an olive green Santa Claus, he said, "No one wants the cities, right?"

"Couldn't agree more."

"Speaking of cities, have you been to Fort Irwin?"

"Just came from there."

"Amazing how that town survived, isn't it? The Rift literally side-swiped it. Did you visit the crack house?"

"I did. Took that frightening step out the back door."

"Good for you. Some folks won't do it. Well, I should let you get back to it. Enjoy your visit. My last name is Wilson, in case you ever want to do an article about me."

"I'll remember that, Ranger Dan Wilson. Thanks."

Even though filtered by the trees, the sunlight was far too bright in Arcon's apartment. He wasn't accustomed to seeking sleep in the afternoon. But he'd never attempted to rise in darkness either.

He thought about hanging a goat hide over the window, but that would signal to everyone in the south courtyard that something was out of place. He never covered his window.

Arcon knew it wasn't just the light. Anticipation was keeping his mind far too active. He rolled out of bed and strode to his desk. The light was good for reading, so once again he opened the journal.

The impenetrable barrier around ArcPoint may be the needle-brush, but that wasn't what had initially trapped the Community. It was the earth cracks that had cut off travel to the outside world. He flipped through the journal to find information about that point in time:

> *Thank God the Facility stood. There was so much noise when the earthquake hit I was convinced it was coming down around us. Everything's a mess, but everyone's alive. Thank you, Jesus.*
>
> *We've been cleaning up for a month, and I finally have a moment to write in this thing again. I need to at least record the highlights of the latest events and think through how we're going to proceed.*
>
> *I thought we were far enough from the San Andreas that we wouldn't experience such a shaking. Hard to believe the earth broke in half less than 30 miles down the freeway from us. They're calling it a rift of some sort. We won't be getting out of here that direction any time soon.*

Herb took his Land Rover for a drive to see what our options are to get to civilization. There is another bad earth crack on the I-15 between here and Baker, and Crucero road has some scary spots along it. Only four-wheel drives can go that way.

Looks to me like we only have two options. Either we abandon this place while we still can, or we set it up for long-term survival. Abandonment would crush those of us who have poured our lives into this project. Some have sold everything and have nowhere else to go.

I'll talk to the ones who put up the lease money first. Then we'll gather everyone together to see if we have what it takes to survive. Meanwhile, I'll send someone to find out what's going on with the earthquakes. It may not be safe for us to stay.

It was obvious to Arcon they stayed, but he wasn't sure of the reason. The next few entries dealt with other matters. One entry was started but crossed out. On the following page he found why they decided to stay:

The tectonic report is confusing, but encouraging. The experts don't know when the rift formation will end, so no clue when the earthquakes will stop. Good news is, we are located on the stable side of it—what they call the deformed Craton—so the worst shaking should be over. We'll just need to keep stuff tied down.

The rail line is still intact east of our location, but that may not last. Union Pacific is scrambling to build another connector to BNSF near the Nevada border. They're tearing up the track through our area for materials to build the new line. They've agreed to leave the track that's on our land.

We have a crew in Vegas loading up rail cars with anything we can think of so we can live here indefinitely. Extra clothes, camping gear, and survival food are pretty obvious. But Norm bought thousands of seed packets and hydroponic garden supplies. Solar panels, chemistry supplies, metal and woodworking tools. The list keeps growing. Union Pacific will deliver the cars, but we have only weeks to be ready.

The decision to stay wasn't unanimous. A few have chosen to leave. It appears we'll end up with about 300 who believe God wants us here and will help us survive. But like the Israelites leaving Egypt, we need to grab everything we possibly can as we go.

Arcon didn't have that luxury. Everything he needed had to be on his back, or already stashed in a cache along the way. He'd have to grab more food on his way out. And get some sleep, if he could. He closed the journal and crawled back in bed.

CHAPTER SEVEN

WEDNESDAY

Arcon quietly stuffed his pack long before daylight. He included nothing the forest could provide, but the pack still seemed heavy. Under normal circumstances he'd restock at the Sunset Outpost, but that would be dangerous.

The rain overnight was perfect: just enough so swinging was discouraged, but still possible. The other hunters would sleep in, giving him a few hours head start.

Arcon's silenced cuckoo clock read four fifteen. Considering he'd checked it nearly every hour through the night, he felt quite rested. As unreliable as it was, he wished he didn't have to leave it behind. It had been a favorite possession of his grandma, given to her by Victoria Franklin. Then he saw a rock on his desk. Jarden had given him that rock when he was young. Arcon polished it and gave it to his grandma. *With this I'll remember them both.* He tucked it in a safe spot in his pack.

He stepped out of his apartment and over to the second floor railing, checking for movement below. He tested the tranquility of the Facility with a quick trip to the kitchen. He grabbed dried meat and fruit, and a couple handfuls of hazelnuts. He saw a small block of goat cheese and grabbed it, then snuck back to his apartment.

Stuffing these recent supplies into his pack, he drank as much water as he could so he wouldn't need to carry it. Then he threw the pack over his shoulders and strapped it on. It would be out of place to wear it indoors, but if he was spotted he could run faster with it on.

He glanced around and slowly opened the door. He avoided the squeaky step on the stairway and crept through the Facility, exiting out the south entrance. Standing under the cover, he scanned for activity, and then looked towards the forest. There was a fog in the trees. But the clouds were thin and the moon beyond was full. It would be too dark to see the trail, so he'd have the advantage if he were chased. He could do it with his eyes closed.

His first goal was the Sowester Swingway. The traps were recently worked on this route, so no one should notice he'd used one set of the ropes. To confuse someone trying to track him, he'd head south as far as he could, then sneak through the forest to the Sowester. By the time he got to that set of ropes, it should be light enough to swing.

For years he and Jarden had brainstormed how to leave the ArcPoint forest. When Jarden was young, it had still been possible, with many open pathways. But now there was a wall of needle-brush in every direction, and you had to climb into the trees to get above it.

Jarden never showed a desire to leave the Community, but he seemed to enjoy discussing the logistics of it. Looking on a map, the simplest route was to head north on the old roadway until you got to the I-15 freeway. But then it was over a hundred miles to any civilization they knew of. They had no vehicles or animals to haul supplies. It just didn't make sense.

Jarden thought the best route was to the south, but it would take an army of machetes to accomplish it. Scouts would have to locate a path through the earth cracks. Then it was still sixty miles to get around the end of the Rift. Which was precisely why Arcon would head south as expected, to deceive them. Then he'd go toward the Rift, which was only twenty miles away. With Elaina helping him, it was the wisest course of action.

His entire plan hinged on getting past the far ridge before anyone discovered him or his secret swingway. If he did, no one could catch him. He was sure of that. He pulled the hood of his goat-hide jacket over his head and made a run for it.

Raymo was just coming around the corner of the Facility when he saw a dark figure at the South entrance. He was about to yell a greeting when the person ran for the woods, which made little sense. There weren't any homes in that direction, and this was neither the time nor the weather for a hunter to be heading for the forest.

Raymo needed to alert somebody. He started for the south entrance, but waking everyone may only get him in trouble. People were kidding him about taking his new night security job too seriously. But he was certain he'd seen some kind of machine in the night sky just two nights ago. Raymo decided to wake his boss and let him give the commands. He turned and ran west toward the log homes.

Where the moon lit Raymo's path he was fine. But at the forest's edge he remembered one of his jobs was to watch for coyotes. He wanted to run, but it was just too dark to see the path, and if he took the wrong one he'd wake the wrong person. At this time of the night all the log homes looked alike. He took it slow and easy.

Raymo's fear subsided when he found the home of his boss, Keenan Phillips. He knocked on the door, waited, and knocked again. He counted to twenty and knocked again. His boss was a stickler for protocol. Now he was to wait a couple minutes, and if no one came to the door, he was to pound on it if it was important, or leave if it wasn't. He wasn't about to leave alone.

Just as he clenched his fist to start pounding, the door opened. "Mr. Phillips, I just saw something I need to tell you about," Raymo blurted.

Keenan Phillips sighed. "What is it, another flying machine?"

"No, I—"

"A major plumbing leak in hydroponics?"

"I didn't see any."

"Is something on fire?"

"No, nothing like that."

"Then what else could be important enough to wake me before first light?"

"I just saw someone run into the woods."

"So?"

"Sir, it's four something in the morning, it's raining, and he was headed south."

Keenan was quiet for a moment. "None of that makes sense."

"That's what I thought. That's why I'm here."

"Did you see who it was?"

"I was too far away, but I'm sure it was a man. He was big, and..."

"What is it?"

"I think he was carrying something on his back."

"Probably a hunter's pack. There are two swingways that direction."

"Not down *that* trail. I'm saying he went *straight* out from the door."

"Tell you what. Go find Bill Winters. He'd know if any of the hunters had a special task to perform. Beyond that, I don't know what to tell you. Check around in the Facility and make sure everything's okay. Come get me if there seems to be anything out of order. Actually..." Keenan's face contorted in thought. "Ahhhh, all right. I won't be able to sleep now, anyway. Let me get dressed. I'll meet you at the South entrance."

"I can stay and walk with you."

"No, get to the Facility and check it out. It's highly unlikely, but it may have been an outsider. Just look things over for a while and I'll see you inside the south door."

Arcon felt his right leg slide out from under him. By instinct he threw himself face down, plunging his bone-handled knife into the ground. He continued a slow slide, but the knife held and stopped him. Lifting his head, he struggled to figure out what had happened.

In the glow of the moonlit clouds, Arcon could see the silhouette of the trees, but not the trail under them. He crawled back up to level ground and got to his feet. As he got his bearings, he realized he'd stepped off corner number seven, where the trail turned east. He was sure he'd counted his paces, but the corner had come five sooner than expected. He must be taking longer strides than when he paced with his eyes closed.

He'd been heading toward the South Swingway, not bothering to hide his footprints. He'd now passed the turnoff to Sowester, hoping to keep any trackers headed away from there. They would see where he walked off the trail. *Maybe that's a good thing.* He quickly reworked his plan to include that evidence.

Looking up, he spotted the tree he needed. It was on the west side of the trail and had a branch that crossed to the east. This was the point where he'd change course towards the Sowester.

He followed the main trail east onto a rock outcropping. Once his moccasins no longer left tracks, he circled back through the underbrush to the branch he'd spotted. He jumped up, grabbed the branch, and pulled himself onto it.

The forest canopy here was sparse enough for him to barely see the branch, so he walked along it to the trunk of the tree, crossing over the path below. Now he was headed west, and anyone tracking him should be following the path east. Or maybe they'd search where he slipped off the path. Either way, it should keep them busy for a while.

Crawling around the trunk, he climbed onto another branch on the opposite side. He walked as far out as he dared, hoping to see something familiar. To his right he saw the branch he needed to be on and the tree he was to jump to. He ran back to the trunk, out the correct branch, then leaped to the next tree.

He felt a burst of fear when his feet met the branch. Only one foot landed on it. He instinctively threw his arms out, dropped to a crouch, and waited for the branch and his heart to calm down.

He straightened and realized he'd done it. His plan to deceive was finished. Now he needed to seal it. He progressed quickly along the branches, moving far from the trail so no one would see or hear his movements. Before long he had backtracked ten trees toward the Sowester Trail.

Below, the ground dropped down a slope, and the needle brush grew dense. But the branches of other trees were below him as well. He spotted a good heavy one not too far down and jumped without giving it much thought. Before the branch stopped bouncing, he ran across it to the trunk.

He sat on the branch to rest, to hide, and to plan his next moves through unknown territory. He knew there were two ravines to get across. Dropping into them wouldn't be difficult. If he missed a branch, he'd land on the next, just like a squirrel.

Traveling uphill was more difficult. He'd have to climb high up a tree, just to hit a low branch on the next one. He'd done it before, but in a brighter light, and with a partner to help him if things didn't go as planned. In this rocky area he had to be especially careful. Crashing into briars was painful, but at least they would break your fall, not your neck.

If he had to, he'd wait for more light. *No reason to hurry. No one will be awake for hours.*

CHAPTER EIGHT

Raymo stood with Keenan at the South entrance to the Facility. "Okay, when I first saw him he was standing right here. Before I could yell a greeting, he ran off in that direction."

Keenan stared at the forest. "I have to agree, that doesn't make sense. It had to have been a hunter or an outsider. You better wake up Bill Winters and see what he knows."

Raymo went to Bill Winters' home and informed him of what he'd seen. Bill walked to the Facility with him, left him and Keenan in the dining hall, and went to Jarden's apartment.

It surprised Raymo they took him seriously. He'd caused a major upset over a buzzing noise in the sky just two days ago. His yelling woke half the people in the Facility, none of whom heard what he had said.

The noise must be related to this incident. An invasion must be starting! First the outsiders sent in a spying machine. We didn't defend ourselves, so now they've sent a spy. That has to be the answer.

As Raymo waited with Keenan in the dining room, he wondered what was taking place with Bill and Jarden. They'd talked near Jarden's apartment, then disappeared for a while. Now they were walking down the stairs. They didn't look happy.

As they approached, Jarden glanced his direction and nodded. Raymo rose from his chair to meet them, but Jarden shook his head and pointed to Keenan. He sat down and Keenan went to talk with them.

Raymo couldn't hear what they were saying, but the conversation looked animated. They glanced in his direction once but then went back to talking amongst themselves.

Raymo fidgeted but kept quiet. He knew he'd done nothing wrong, except maybe wake someone for no reason. In fact, his actions may be the very thing that would give the Community a chance to defend itself. His patience was waning by the time they came back.

Jarden spoke first. "Raymo, we want to thank you for alerting us to this situation. We need to check out a few things before we know for sure what's going on, so we'd like you to keep this incident between us."

Raymo stiffened. "You want me to keep it secret from everyone?"

"You know we don't keep secrets," answered Jarden. "But we also don't spread rumors, and right now we don't know enough to relay the facts. We just ask that you follow the chain of command. Keenan will keep you informed of what we find. Hopefully, we'll know more in the next hour or two."

"I'm fine with that," said Raymo. "But if you have any idea what, or who, I saw, please let me know." He turned to Keenan. "I still have about two hours of security rounds. Shall I keep doing that while I wait?"

"That would be perfect, Raymo," said Keenan. "Feel free to check with me whenever you want, and let us know if you see or hear anything else. I'll look you up as soon as we know something."

"Thanks boss. I'll go pump water in hydroponics again. See you later."

Arcon reached familiar territory near the trail heading toward the Sowester swingway. To make sure his footprints wouldn't be found, he walked the tree branches as far as he could alongside the trail. It was getting light, so he dropped to the trail and began running. When he reached the Sowester swingway, he could see well enough to swing.

From this point he would swing the Sowester to just short of the Outpost. He'd then crawl through the needle brush on a hidden trail to his newly constructed swingway. He put on his official bright yellow hunter vest. If a hunter spotted him, they'd whistle a customary greeting and assume he was out hunting. He'd respond as if nothing was wrong, but know he'd been seen.

He didn't think any hunters would be suspicious. They knew he did this sort of thing. But part way down the new swingway he would need to remove his vest and sneak to his secret section of swings. A spot of bright yellow arcing across Far Ridge would be an obvious attention grabber. He hoped to be past it before anyone woke up.

He said a quick prayer for eyes to see the branches, for strength to last the day, and for hands to get a grip. Nothing could stop him now. He grabbed the first rope of the Sowester swingway and was tempted to snag the other. If neither of the ropes were there to swing on, the other hunters would have to work hard to get to them. They would waste precious time in the dangerous needle-brush, giving him a needed advantage. They'd never catch him—and they'd never forgive him. He couldn't do it.

Jumping off the branch he felt the tug of extra weight from the pack, and the wind blowing through his scraggly beard and long hair. He had the strange perception that God was helping push him, and Elaina was pulling him, and that what he was doing was right.

Chad awoke to a knock on his apartment door. He glanced out the window. It was just barely getting light so he couldn't have overslept. Chad yelled, "Just a minute." From the edge of his bed, he pulled on his night-robe. He heard Bill Winters voice. "It's just me and Jarden."

"Oh. Okay. Come on in." Chad stretched his shoulders till they popped and ran his hand over his short hair. As the men walked in, he asked, "What brings you around at this time of the morning?"

As he closed the door, Jarden said, "We have a job for you, one you're uniquely qualified for."

"Uh oh. The last time you said that I had to slaughter a goat. That wasn't any fun."

"No, no. This involves nothing dying. I hope."

Chad saw Jarden's stern expression and realized it hadn't been a joke. "I'm not sure I like the sound of *that* either."

"No, and you probably won't find this job fun. I need you to track somebody."

"Somebody, or some *thing?*"

"We need you to track Arcon. You know what his footprints look like, don't you?"

"Well, of course, but … he's probably in his room sleeping. I just talked to him yesterday."

"Well, he's not in his room and neither is his backpack. We think Raymo saw him run into the woods while it was still dark."

"What? That doesn't make sense. Why would he do that?"

"You've heard him talk about leaving the Community before, haven't you?"

"A long time ago, yeah. But he hasn't talked about that in many moons."

Jarden hesitated, not wanting to betray Arcon's trust. But his first loyalty was to the Community. "We discussed it a couple days ago. I thought I'd talked him out of it. Can you get dressed and meet us at the south entrance? I want to see if you recognize Arcon's footprints there."

"Sure, sure. I'll just be a minute."

Jarden stood with Bill and Keenan. They watched Chad examine the ground. "Arcon's definitely been here recently. Those long, skinny feet are easy to spot. Looks like he's carrying more weight than usual." He looked at Keenan. "Which way did Raymo see him go?"

Keenan pointed to the trail leading into the woods. "Straight out from the door."

"We tie up the goats out that direction, but if we want to go to a swingway, we take the main trail to the east, and not through that rocky ground." He walked a few yards in the direction Keenan had pointed. "You're right. His tracks go right through here. Why would he do that?"

"Because it would slow us down," remarked Jarden. "This would be a shortcut to either the South or the Sowester swingways. Over the rocky areas he'd be hard to track."

"But why not just take the main trail?"

"Before dawn?" asked Jarden.

Chad looked toward the forest. "Oh, I see what you mean. The main trail has a canopy. Would've been pitch black."

"Would you mind trying to track him? Bill, you take the main trail around to where the Sowester splits off. See if you can find Arcon's tracks."

"What if it's too dark?"

"Then follow the main trail around to the South swingway. It should be light enough to tell if one of those lines of swings has been used."

"And if I can't?"

Jarden realized Bill wasn't used to the forest like the hunters were. "Wait for Chad where the trail splits. Then one of you can go toward the Easter Outpost and whistle Danner and Sander to help. Keenan, you can stay here in case he comes back. Just in case, I'm going to head toward the Sunset Outpost."

"He wouldn't go that way, would he?" asked Bill. "Toward the Rift? That'd be suicidal."

"I don't think he'd go that way either. But Derik and Tawny are out there. I'll have Tawny try to find Arcon's new swingway.

It's supposed to start somewhere around the Sunset Outpost. We should be able to tell if he used it."

"Look southeast," said Chad.

"Have you been to it?"

"No, not yet. But when Arcon worked on it, he'd hike down the hill to the southeast from the Outpost. He'd climb a big tree, then run full tilt and leap to another tree, with a coil of rope over his shoulder. I never had the nerve to follow him. Plus, you have to be as tall as he is just to climb the first tree."

"Okay, thanks. I'll put Tawny to work looking for it."

"Sounds good, Jarden," said Chad. "I'm heading out to track him."

"Me too," said Bill.

"Good, but realize something," said Jarden. "We still don't know his true motive. We may be getting all worked up for nothing, so we just need to find him and talk with him."

"Do you want us to question him?" asked Chad. "Or leave that up to you?"

"It won't hurt to ask him," said Jarden. "But tell him I want to talk with him. And remember, we're doing this to make sure Arcon doesn't get hurt out there. So I don't want aggressive confrontation, or any of you risking your lives. If it gets too dangerous, just let him go, and pray for him. Understood?"

As Raymo returned from the hydroponics building, he saw the four men standing where he'd witnessed the person running into the woods. Jarden was pointing in different directions, and Chad was staring at the ground. Raymo went to join the conversation, but the group dispersed as he approached. *Are they avoiding me?*

He trailed Jarden and Keenan into the building, but when they went in different directions, he chased after Keenan. As he got alongside, he whispered, "Did you find anything?"

Keenan stopped. Not seeing anyone else within earshot he answered, "We're convinced the person you saw was Arcon. Chad has verified his footprints, and we have a plan forming to track him down. But we still don't know why Arcon ventured out at night. Until we know, let's stick to the plan and not spread rumors. Give us a couple days to find Arcon and question him. Then we'll have some understanding of how best to address the situation."

"Don't you think people need to know *something?*"

"If it had been an outsider, I would agree with you. But this is one of our own, and he deserves to be considered righteous until proven otherwise."

"I agree to your terms, boss. But please keep me informed of what's happening. I think certain people need to understand the situation."

Keenan's brow furrowed. "Raymo, I especially don't want you saying anything to the Ashford's. Not until we know the facts. Understood?"

Raymo felt his face flush. He hadn't thought his intentions toward Brina were that obvious. "Yes sir, understood."

"Alright then. You have a couple more hours until you're relieved. If you need me, I'll be in the shop working on a project. See you later."

"See you, boss."

Raymo was relieved it hadn't been an outsider. *Who knows what kind of weapons the outside world has now.* He'd glanced through many books in the room of Ancient Evil and read about horrific confrontations between both good and evil men. It was likely things had only gotten worse.

Part of him hoped they'd never find Arcon. With him out of the picture, maybe Brina would look his direction more often. He'd moved from the clothing building to hydroponics so he could see her more. But her parents didn't seem to enjoy talking with him.

He pictured Brina crying on his shoulder, upset by what Arcon had done. It was a comforting thought.

Jarden walked into the Room of Remembrance and went straight to the maps. He stared at the crayon marks that showed the routes of the swingways. He knew Arcon was trying to connect the Sunset and Sowester outposts with his new swingway. But that new route would do nothing to help him get out of ArcPoint.

For years they'd discussed possible ways out, but Jarden had always used those conversations to explain how impossible it was. *Arcon, what are you thinking?*

He had to go south. Jarden had gone that direction often as a young man. But time had changed the landscape. He'd never risk it now. If Arcon went that way, he'd have to let him go. The more he stared at the map, the more it seemed Arcon might head to the Rift. The new swingway must have something to do with it. A thought came to him, and he hurried out the door, heading for the Sunset Outpost.

CHAPTER NINE

Arcon sailed past the briars, letting go of the rope before even touching the branch. As soon as he landed, he moved swiftly to the opposite side of the tree. His stealth was in vain if anyone spotted him on Far Ridge. It was time to hide the vest until he needed Elaina to see it. He tucked it inside his backpack and scrambled down to the ground.

He could hear their whistles. They'd tracked him to the Sowester. *How could they have found out so quickly?* They'd know he was no longer headed south, but if no one had spotted him, they wouldn't expect him this close to the Sunset Outpost. They'd be searching in the wrong area for hours.

Swing time was over. Now his travels would be slow and painful, but he was driven. He wanted to meet Elaina. She seemed to have his same passion for adventure.

He knew the stories about the ancient evil that had consumed the outside world, but he sensed nothing evil about Elaina. Like Jarden, Arcon believed Jesus had returned and removed the evil nature of man, and the ArcPoint Community didn't realize it.

If the devil and his evil spirits still existed, he was prepared to resist them. In all the years he'd been communicating with Elaina, never once had he received caution within, only the peace his grandma told him was from God.

For the others, God's peace was in this forest. But for him, true peace was out *there* somewhere. The Community needed to let him find it.

Derik balanced on the treetop platform looking through his binoculars. He'd seen something from the corner of his eye he assumed was a bird. But when Jarden arrived at the outpost, his recollection took a different turn. What he thought he'd seen was vest colored.

He scanned the area, looking for signs of Arcon. If he was wearing the vest, as required by the Community, it should be simple enough to spot him on that rocky hillside. There was just one problem. That was the base of Far Ridge, and it was off-limits to the hunters.

Then his well-trained eye spotted a vertical streak of color unlike any other in the area. A hanging hemp rope. He scanned a full swing-length around that area and found another. Then another. And another. "I think I've spotted where he went," he said to Jarden. Derik handed the nocs to Jarden on the branch below. "Right through there you'll see a series of ropes. How did he build that swingway without us noticing?"

"The kid's resourceful. Gotta give him that."

"Do we dare send the hunters out to Far Ridge?"

Jarden handed the nocs back. "Call them here and we'll discuss it."

Almost reluctantly Derik let out a shrill, piercing whistle to gather the other hunters. They responded with different whistles. Derik interpreted. "Chad just now got to the Sowester Outpost. He's going back to get the rest of them."

"That means they could all be there soon," said Jarden.

"What should I tell them?"

Jarden stared at the area where the ropes hung. "Send Chad back to the split. He and Bill can hike around to Sunset; the others can take the Sowester to the Outpost. Arcon may be headed for that low spot in the ridge. We'll try to get there before him."

Just then they saw Tawny climbing the tree toward them. "What did you find?" asked Derik.

"I found Arcon's swingway, but it hasn't been used," said Tawny. "It only has one set of ropes and they're ready to use from this side."

Derik turned to Jarden. "Speaking of that, all the ropes on the Sunset swingway are faced this direction."

"I'll reset one for them," said Jarden.

"Are you sure?" asked Derik. "Tawny could do that."

"I suppose you're right. But I'd almost forgotten how fun it is." He turned to Tawny. "Use Arcon's swingway to go back toward the Sowester. Since Arcon came this direction, it must connect somewhere, probably near the Outpost. Have the others search for a hidden swingway. We see one going toward Far Ridge. It must start near Arcon's new one." Turning to Derik, he said, "Send the signals to make that all work."

Derik's face went blank. He moved his fingers in the air as if tracking their movements. "Okay! Got it. I can do that."

"Great. I'll see you in a few."

Arcon was just approaching the location of his cache when he heard a whistle. It was Derik, gathering the hunters. Then another—Chad saying he'd reached his destination and was returning. *Why had he responded like that?*

Arcon ducked under a rhizome and continued down his crude trail. He heard more whistles and stopped. The first indicated the message was for Chad, *Go to Sunset*. Then, Bill, *Go to Sunset*. The whistling paused. Arcon started to move, then stopped. Another series of whistles said, *Send help to Sowester Outpost*. None of that made sense to Arcon. Maybe it wasn't supposed to.

Continuing toward his cache of supplies he heard another whistle. A call to meet at the Sunset Outpost, directed at him.

The proper protocol was to acknowledge the whistle, but that would give away his location. *Smart thinking Derik.*

He ignored the message, but agonized over making the other hunters travel through needle brush. Survival, either his own or someone else's, was normally the only motivation for facing inch-long thorns. He wished he could make them want to give up.

His heart sank when he saw a hole where his cache should be. *Coyotes.* Now he wished he'd rationed his supplies better. But his pursuers probably weren't prepared to overnight in the woods like he was. When the sun got low they'd head to the outpost. No one traveled through needle brush in the dark.

There was a belief among the ArcPoint dwellers that the forest ended not far beyond the ridge he was on. No one but Jarden had ever made it this far.

His well-made plan was falling apart. He needed to be further west, or he'd have to cross the ridge. If he did that, he may never find Wilhelm Wash. He'd have to wander blindly, knowing only that the Rift was west and the I-15 was north. He needed to shake the hunters off his trail.

His height gave him the advantage. He looked around and saw a large tree just ahead. He hacked the briars until he got to one of its branches. *Perfect.* He jumped up and grabbed it, pulling and twisting until he was sitting on it. *None of them are tall enough to do that. They'll have to find their own tree, or make a trail.*

He looked around. *They won't know where to go.* He ran down the branch, climbed higher, then chose another going toward a tree that was unreachable. He had a plan that was sure to discourage them. He could beat them to the other side of Far Ridge. Derik wouldn't let them follow. *Lord, please don't let them follow. For their own sake, persuade them to let me go.*

❖

"Dan, did you hear what I just said?"

"What was that?" Dan Wilson looked at his wife's inquisitive face and realized she'd asked a question. "I'm sorry. What did you just say?"

"Well, you answered that question. Now I'll repeat the first one, provided I have your attention."

"I'm all ears, honey."

"I need to go visit my sister in Oregon. Are you going to be okay without me for a while? I'll be gone a week or so."

"Is she still remodeling her kitchen?"

"She's almost done. She wants my input on decorating. You know how she is. She just needs a little help making decisions."

"I'll be fine. I could stand to lose a few pounds anyway."

"Oh, no you don't. I expect you to feed yourself. And don't go visiting your mom just to get a meal." She looked closely at him and sensed he wasn't his normal jovial self. "Is something bothering you?"

"Aaaahh, it's no big deal. I just had some visitors at the station asking about the Mojave People again."

"You get that all the time. Why did it bother you today?"

"They were discussing all the rumors ... how the Mojave People are like wild animals. I had to take the official position and say that no one knows, so we need to maintain a separation. But in my heart it felt like a lie. I feel like the Mojave People are my children, and it hurts to hear people talk bad about them."

"I think God wants you to have room in your heart for the Mojave People. Maybe someday you'll get your chance to visit them. Just don't do it while I'm on my trip, because I'd like to go with you."

"Okay, I promise I'll wait for you to get back."

"It's a deal."

CHAPTER TEN

Elaina walked out to her small three-wheel autocycle. She opened the trailer, removed the rescue drone, and set it on the concrete pavers of the driveway. Then she wrestled out all the components for the portable shelter. Protection from weather was nice to have during a rescue, but on this trip she needed to be mobile. And she didn't want to be in a structure with *San Bernardino Search and Rescue* splashed all over it.

With the shelter removed, there was space for the high-powered telescope and digital camera gear. The cabin would put them ten kilometers from where Arcon should appear. With this scope, she wouldn't have to pace along the Rift every day with binoculars. She normally stored the telescope in the back seat for rescues. But now she hoped to use that space for a worn out escapee from the Mojave Forest.

With the scope secured, she repacked the controls, tools, drone and its cradle into the trailer. She'd done this dozens of times before, but never was as emotionally attached to a rescue as she was now.

Her job with San Bernardino Search and Rescue was to keep and maintain the drone. It was also her responsibility to deliver it to rescue sites and to fix it when necessary. It was no accident she had this job. She'd begged for it. So had her father. Thankfully, he'd had the clout to make it happen.

She stared at the drone, remembering how she enjoyed spending time with her dad. She'd been barely a teenager when her mother died in a tragic accident. When she wasn't in school, she'd be with her dad, which often included going along on rescue missions.

She'd learned to stay out of the way, and eventually to help. She'd spent hours watching someone use the drone to locate and assist lost or injured hikers. One day she spotted something others had missed, and a life was saved. From that day on she was hooked.

While other kids her age watched entertainment devices, Elaina listened to the SBS&R emergency scanner. After a while she'd predict when her dad would be called away to work before he did. She was fourteen when she heard Arcon's SOS signal on the scanner.

At first she didn't know what it was, but could tell by the repetitive nature it was manmade. Her dad recognized the Morse code, something that hadn't been used in regular communications for nearly two hundred years. The strange rhythmic static didn't last long, so her dad told her not to waste time on it. That didn't stop her from listening for it and studying about Morse code.

A month later, she'd once more heard long and short bursts of static. As before, it started with SOS, then changed to other combinations. She'd grabbed a pencil and paper and written down the noise as dots and dashes like she'd seen in a book. When the static stopped, she'd run to her dad, and they worked to make sense of it. Deciphering the message hadn't been easy. But one phrase had come through clearly. *Can anyone hear me?*

Elaina had thought it could be someone trapped in a cave with no other means to communicate. Her dad had said it was probably a kid playing adventure games with a broken radio transmitter, but had seen no harm in setting up listening equipment to triangulate the signal. They'd figure out where it was coming from, just in case that person needed help. Elaina and her dad's lives were changed when they discovered the signal was coming from the Mojave Restricted Area.

They'd assumed it was coming from a long-distance hiker who'd gotten lost. *But why Morse code?* They contacted various authorities, but the answer was the same. It was out of their jurisdiction.

Elaina and her dad shared a passion for rescuing total strangers, but they rarely agreed on how or why they should rescue this particular one. But, together they experimented until they found a way to communicate in code. The first thing they asked was whether the stranger was one of the Mojave People. The answer scared her dad. This person answered, [MAYBE].

Elaina's dad had told her a hiker wouldn't respond in a halfway manner like that. It was common knowledge to anyone doing a multi-day hike in that area; if you see or smell Acacia trees, turn around. On the other hand, the Mojave People may not know the name given to them. Her dad pulled the plug on the radio transmitter.

Elaina, still curious, studied what she could about the Mojave People and the Restricted Area they lived in. When she read they might be infected with the evil spirits of the early twenty-first century, she studied more about those times. It scared her.

The horrors of the tribulation years weren't hidden from people, but no one she asked cared to discuss them. She'd witnessed many tragedies, even death, because of her dad's job. But they were accidents—unexpected and unintentional. Centuries ago people caused harm to themselves and others intentionally, their malicious thoughts instigated by evil spirits.

When Jesus returned, he swept those spirits from the planet and renewed the law that angels were to dwell in Heaven and not visit earth. That should include the Mojave Forest, so she struggled with why it was closed to society. Since Central Authority would give no clear understanding for the restriction, society came up with explanations of its own.

Their reasons were hard to ignore because they were based on Bible verses. The first was *Hosea 2:6 "For this reason I will fence her in with thornbushes. I will block her path with a wall to make her lose her way.*" The wall was obviously the Rift, and Arcon admitted his people created the thornbushes.

Another verse was *Proverbs 22:5 Thorns and snares are in the way of the perverse; He who guards himself will be far from them.* That verse had conveyed such a warning, she agreed with her dad to stop communicating. But the stranger didn't. She still heard that strange code every so often. She couldn't help but decipher it.

She worked to memorize Morse code, although the dots and dashes weren't always clear. She would sneak him a quick message now and then. She found out he was a teenager named Arcon. He lived in a forest, his parents had died, and he lived with his grandmother. He wanted to know about her. She seldom responded. He begged for more.

After years of rejecting Arcon's pleas, he made one that hit her in the heart. His beloved grandmother had died, and he needed someone to talk to, someone on the outside. To do that, she had to confess to her dad about what was going on.

Her dad consented, but only if he could monitor the discussion. He warned her that evil spirits could cause people to lie. Elaina reasoned God would help them discern those spirits if they asked Him to. Over the years, they'd asked many times for God to intervene if Arcon was misleading them. They got no impression Arcon was lying or guided by evil spirits, although they'd never truly spoken with him.

When Arcon talked of escape, she was ready at once; her dad remained reluctant for years. Now the time had come to act, and the drone would play a critical role for getting Arcon across the Rift. That's why she'd worked hard to get this job and always have access to it. She could repair it on the spot with parts she carried in the trailer. No one in the SBS&R could do it faster. She made sure of that.

If this didn't work, she'd be forced to tell the authorities about Arcon and let them decide. She knew they'd follow the rules and leave him in the Mojave.

Over time, she'd gotten to know Arcon, sort of. She was sure they were both following what God was asking them to do. For that reason alone she was willing to push the limits of the rules and risk putting her fate in the hands of the judges.

Elaina locked the trailer. An alert tone squawked from the phone attached to her shoulder. A series of notes identified her dad as the caller. She said, "Yes," so the phone would connect. "Hi Dad."

"Hi girl, how's it going?"

"Just packed the telescope and drone. Going to grab some lunch. Were you able to get the roll-up screen?"

"No, it's still out in the field. You'll have to monitor the scope with your laptop."

"Can you get it by this weekend?"

"It'll be back tomorrow. They know we want to use it for, you know, testing the drone. So unless there's an emergency, I'll be there with it Friday night."

"Get there earlier if you can. It'll be hard to see much without the big screen."

"Understood. Now you have room for more stuff."

"I'll fill it with something."

"I know you will, girl. See you tonight."

"Later Big D." She tapped the phone to end the call. She knew she couldn't complain, but losing the screen was a blow to her plans.

Instead of going to the kitchen, she collapsed in the front room in her recliner and went through her checklist. She had personal ropes and climbing equipment; her dad would bring the rest. Survival food and plenty of fluids for Arcon. Medical supplies just in case. Food for her and her dad. Clothes, toiletries, snacks, sunscreen, and breath mints. The drone was in the trailer, and the backseat of her autocycle was half-full. Nothing to do now but try to think of what else she could fill it with.

◆

Derik was getting frustrated with the hunters' slow progress. He was guiding as best he could with standard directional whistles. But the trees toward Far Point were sparse and the needle brush was dense. Arcon had swung past what was now slowing his hunters. He looked down and saw Jarden climbing up to join him in the Lookout.

"How's it going?" asked Jarden.

"We were so close," said Derik. "The guys found the hidden swingway and they're working their way to the end of it. I hate to say it, but I think I just spotted Arcon headed up the ridge."

"He must have figured out our plan to cut him off. Call Bill and Sander back. Our best shot is for the guys to find whatever path he took once he ran out of ropes. Are they close to the last one you spotted?"

Looking closely, Derik could see there were no other ropes beyond the latest one the hunters located. He whistled a signal that meant *halt and observe.*

Danner, the eldest of the hunters, heard the whistle, letting them know they were close. He yelled, "See if there are any ropes we haven't swung with."

They all looked around, agreeing the most recent rope was the last. "Okay," said Danner, "Determine where his landing point was. He'll be on foot now, either running branches or fighting the needle-brush. This is where we'll catch him."

"He can outrun all of us on branches," said Chad.

"He won't have many," responded Danner. "He'll have to make a trail. He'll slow to a snail's pace and wear himself out. All we have to do is follow his trail, but we've gotta find it. Let's hustle before it gets dark."

"That tree—" yelled Tawny, signaling a young student hunter quite astute for his age. "Arcon would've swung higher than we did. He would've landed on that branch right there."

Danner studied that geometry. Since he was located near the branch Tawny referred to, he moved to the tree and climbed. He yelled, "Get that rope up to me." Once the rope was in his hand, he yelled, "I'm going to try it." Danner jumped as high as he could to imitate Arcon's swing and sailed through the trees. At the end of the arc he couldn't quite reach a large branch to jump, but didn't need to—he could see where Arcon had landed. "Check the base of that tree."

The hunters searched for signs of Arcon. Danner let loose a high-pitched cry to let Derik know they'd found something.

When Derik heard the alert, he looked at the sun. They were running out of time. None of them were equipped to spend the night in the ArcPoint Forest. He turned to Jarden. "If we don't find him soon, I'll need to call it off."

"I agree," said Jarden. "Arcon had to have planned this for a long time. I'm sure he's prepared for what's coming. Your boys aren't."

"When the sun moves ten degrees, I'll whistle them back. We can camp at the outpost."

"Will we all fit?"

Derik shrugged his broad shoulders. "It'll be cozy."

"When Bill gets here I'll send him back to the Facility. We shouldn't need him. He's no hunter, anyway."

CHAPTER ELEVEN

Arcon listened. He recognized Danner's last whistle. The hunters had found his trail. Now they would struggle with needle brush and discuss whether to let him go. More worrisome were the two hunters vests he'd seen west of him. He wouldn't be able to get to the Wilhelm Wash with them there. He'd have to climb the ridge.

He was keeping his pace up when he heard another whistle calling the hunters back to the Sunset Outpost for the night. After dusk no one could see to swing, run branches, or avoid thorns, so all travel would end, including his own. Hunters would move at first light, as they had done for over forty years.

Arcon looked for a level place to spend the night. He'd just crested the ridge. If he dropped down the hill a little farther, they couldn't spot a fire. He'd been chased too far south. Now he was amid rugged rock, instead of skirting the edge of it.

Walking along the edge of a boulder, he spotted a gully below. Climbing down and walking on it, he found a spot clear of stones large enough to sleep on. It must have been collecting water and leaves for decades because it had good, level soil. With no branches overhead, it had escaped berry seeds being dropped from birds. *Perfect.*

He scrambled to set up his small campsite, with a makeshift fire pit and leaves for bedding. He'd keep the fire small. There should be no dangerous animals to worry about. They didn't like the dense needle brush that surrounded these hills or the exposure of barren rocks. If there were, the crunch of dead leaves and twigs would warn him of their approach.

He'd never been afraid of the coyotes. He'd seen them from the trees, but they always seemed to flee at the sight of humans. Jarden had warned him about wolves near the Rift. He hoped they were as docile as the coyotes. Jarden said they were vicious, but he may have said that to keep Arcon away from the Rift.

His stomach ached. He knew there was food around him. But he risked being seen if he climbed for the fruit there. And it was unwise to eat the food in his pack; he'd need that later. He'd survive until morning, but that thought wouldn't help him get the sleep he needed.

He tried to focus his mind on Elaina—what he knew about her, what she might look like, or what life could be like when shared with someone. But his thoughts kept returning to the world he lived in. The Community valued isolation, but it had become a utopian prison.

He may not be welcome in the outside world, and ArcPoint may not want him back. He'd never felt so alone. *Lord, I need your help to get to the other side. If that's not my place, then help them catch me. If I make it out, and you need me to return, you can tell me later. I'm committed to my plan, based on the times I've tested this call on my life.*

So many times his grandma had asked him, "What's God telling you?" She taught him God speaks in different ways. Sometimes a thought, sometimes a word from the Bible, someone else, or a circumstance. It was okay to question, as long as you were seeking the truth, and not looking for an excuse to reject God's guidance.

He assembled his dew trap to capture water for the next day. Then he located a comfortable tree, plucked the journal from his backpack, and sat down. Turning to where he'd left off, he found this entry:

This decision to stay in the desert will either be a glorious success or a devastating failure. Either way, I need to at least take a few notes.

It started out well, but went south fast. At first we all just wanted a place to hide, maybe for a few years. We were mostly united: We'd stay until God told us to leave. But was the earthquake and rift God's way of saying, RUN?

Our weekly survival discussions turned strangely religious the other night. Our tight band of believers divided into groups with names like Evangelical, Orthodox, Ecclesiastical, and Messianic. They started throwing around big words like Exegesis, Dispensationalism, Premillennialism, and Cessationism. Then it turned ugly with words like Homiletic, Apostasy, and Cult. That's when I lost it.

Many had been believers far longer than me. Some had gone to seminary. Maybe that kind of talk seemed normal to them. I was born and raised atheist, so my brain vapor-locked at hearing those words. Except for one that sounded like 'exit Jesus', the other word that concerned me was the four-letter one: Cult.

I thought of my grandpa who died in Guyana with the Jim Jones cult. Psychiatrists might say that's why I was an atheist and suicidal. But was that why I led a band of people into the wilderness? That thought scared me so bad I cut loose with my own four letter word: STOP!

I'd had enough and told them that. If they were going to drag their religious baggage with them, they could do it without me. But if they were serious about living in peace with one another, then we had to be of one mind. We could only do that if one Holy Spirit guided us all, and evil spirits guided none of us.

I told them all to leave. Go back to their homes. Think it through. Pray about it. Scream about it if they had to. But the next day we would meet again and I would ask them one simple question: What's God telling you?

To be honest, I went home and tried to figure out where I was going next. I'd been looking forward to the challenge of building a survivable community in the middle of nowhere. That's all Norm and I ever discussed. We didn't get the religious ramifications of what was happening in the world. We wanted to leave it all behind, and I'd thought these other folks did as well.

The next meeting was somber. One by one, people came forward to share what God had said to them. Many had never heard God's voice before that night. That surprised me (and them). Testimonies were all a little different, but the basic message was the same. In this place we belong to Him and need to act like it.

Some said God rebuked them for their harsh criticisms, others for silence. Some had a peace about staying, others a fear of leaving. Many said they didn't hear or feel anything, but knew they wanted peace.

They thanked me for sending them to their rooms. I laughed and told them I wasn't their father; I was just another sibling acting as a babysitter. I made a sweeping gesture with my arm and told them all of this stuff we see around us didn't come from Norm or I. I pointed to the sky and said, "It's from Him." That's when Norm yelled "ArcPoint!"

I said, "Yeah, the trees too."

He said, "No, I mean what you just did." He mirrored my gesture, making an arc with his arm and pointing to the sky. "An arc-point." Then he showed me that again and said, "We should do this and say, 'All of this, from Him!' whenever we meet."

Maybe. We'll see. I told them I never want to hear one of those fancy words again. Speak plain English, or show me in the Bible where those words are. I may have only read the Bible through once, but I never saw words like that.

That night we asked God to make us one in His Spirit, drive everything evil from our midst, and never allow it to return. Surround us with an impenetrable barrier of peace. Help us meet our needs away from the world.

Arcon put the journal back in his pack. The words landed in his heart. God had answered their prayer for separation from the world. It made him think again about stepping outside the protection of ArcPoint.

There would be no turning back once he crossed the Rift. Worst of all, he didn't know exactly what Elaina planned to do with him. He hoped Elaina could help him blend into her world, with no one finding out where he'd come from. He must keep ArcPoint protected from the outsiders.

Elaina said she could be in trouble for helping him. What if she got caught? What would the authorities do to her, or to him? If things didn't work out, how could he ever get back to ArcPoint? Would Elaina join him?

Arcon remembered a few words transmitted in Morse code by Elaina. *God said okay.* Whatever happens next, with God's help, it will be okay.

CHAPTER TWELVE

THURSDAY

Arcon awoke with a start. The sky was growing light. Hunters would be back on his trail before the sunlight hit the trees. He had to get moving. He needed to be in the trees. One thing he couldn't do was fall off a branch. Ever. The ridge was riddled with bone shattering rocks.

The ancient maps showed a creek bed at the base of this ridge. ArcPoint trees flourished in creek beds, and their lower branches were large, long, and stiff. However, the availability of water also made the rhizomes grow more than twice Arcon's height. Because tree branches died under needle brush, a hunter had to be taller to reach them, which played to Arcon's advantage. He was also heavier than the others. But when he had sturdier branches, no one could match his speed and agility.

He grabbed the last banana from his pack and studied his surroundings. To the west, a few trees were growing into a briar patch. They wouldn't expect him to go that direction. Looking at the cold charcoal of his campfire, he knew he couldn't hide this spot from the hunters. He had to send them in a different direction than he was headed. He saw some good trees below him, and started walking. *Sorry, boys. Time to fool you once more.*

Arcon grabbed a branch, launched himself onto it, and ran to the trunk. Turning due south, he ran down a branch to another tree and placed a banana peel where they could see it from his campsite. Then he ran the branches back, and returned to his campsite. Gathering up his belongings, he hiked west till he reached the first tree.

He wrapped his arms in rabbit skins, with fur on the inside, then ran the branches of more trees to the west. At the end of one branch, with no more trees to run on, he tucked his arms behind his head and flung himself back, landing on a cluster of needle-brush. He held his tongue as a dozen thorns penetrated his skin.

Acting like giant springs, the vines broke his fall. His pack and leather vest protected his back. But rabbit fur worked best for preventing scratches, not blocking the points of the thorns. Quite a few penetrated his soft leggings, but still better than wearing the weighty chaps.

Most likely, Derik would only give the hunters one more shot at finding him. If they failed to close the distance, they'd hopefully give up. Today, Arcon would take all the risks and needle pokes necessary.

He curled into a ball and rolled across the vines. Sometimes the rhizomes arced high enough to roll under. No one else saw the wisdom of custom fitting leather gloves, which were thin in the palms for gripping and thick on the backs for protection.

He kept rolling, crawling, and occasionally hacking, until he reached a branch low enough to jump to. He thanked God for the next stand of trees. Rolling over thorns was a painful way to travel. He looked back. The needle-brush was springing back into shape, leaving no trail to follow.

Not long after sunrise, Arcon heard the familiar high-pitched whistle of Derik. This noise meant he was in place to observe, but had nothing to report. That was good and bad news for Arcon. Good, that he hadn't been spotted. Bad that they were on his trail.

It sounded like the whistle had come from the top of Far Ridge. Derik must have followed his men and was now high in a tree spotting for them. The hunters would now be on his side of the ridge. He'd have to be careful.

The hunters knew to remain quiet so as not to scare the prey. They would listen for rustling in the brush and watch for movement. They'd pay attention for signs from bunny birds that may fly overhead.

Arcon was no ordinary prey because he knew all the tricks of the hunters. But unlike rabbits who could remain motionless, he had to keep moving. He wished he could run full tilt beneath needle-brush as they did.

Of particular concern were the bunny birds. They would flock over any critter movement they saw in the forest. The rodents they were after thrived in the needle brush where neither hawks nor coyotes could reach them. But overpopulation would drive them into open areas.

Any movement on the ground made the bunny birds curious. The hunters learned to use the actions of these hawks to find areas where rabbits were becoming too numerous for the land to support them. They had different flight patterns depending on what they saw on the ground—including humans.

If Arcon saw the birds, he would hide and stay still, to make the other hunters draw their attention. Then he'd know where *they* were.

Chad and Sander took turns hacking and searching through the needle brush until they found Arcon's trail again. Every time it disappeared, they knew he'd jumped to a branch. Sometimes they had to boost someone up to it. Then they had to figure out where Arcon went next. The hunters took different branch runs until they spotted his tracks, but Arcon had not made it easy.

Meanwhile, Danner and Tawny were running branches and climbing trees. From high in one tree, Danner spotted Arcon's campsite. He whistled for the other hunters, and they all worked their way to the site. When they were together, Chad asked, "Which way do you think he left from here?"

Sander pointed and said, "I still think he has to be headed south. Probably through that stand of trees."

They all looked that direction. While the others looked around, Danner stared at those trees. Then he climbed up the hill behind him. "I see something."

"What is it?" asked Sander.

"It's something yellow." He walked in that direction until he got to a tree. "Tawny, give me a boost."

Tawny cupped his hands. Danner stepped into them and was launched up to the branch. He walked to the trunk of the tree and glanced around. When he looked toward the south, he said, "I've spotted it. It's definitely yellow."

"Arcon's vest?" asked Chad.

"No, too small." He walked down the branch toward another tree and said, "It's a banana peel. He must have stopped to eat it." Danner jumped to a branch on that tree and walked down it. "Yup. Looks freshly peeled, too. He can't be far. Chad, come down here. There are a few different ways he could have gone. Guys, boost him up."

Toward midday Arcon noticed the trees grew shorter. He was approaching the edge of the forest sooner than expected. Short trees meant less cover and fewer branches to run. He'd planned on crossing to the larger trees at the bottom of the ravine, but he didn't dare, knowing Derik would be watching for him. He didn't want to keep going west. It would take him further from the best point to get to the I-15.

He was already tiring of all this hacking and jumping, running and dropping and hacking again. He wanted to rest and think and plan. He desperately wanted to hear Derik's high-pitched whistle, calling off the hunt. Then he could go north and get back on his mapped route.

Thursday afternoon, Elaina drove off in her three-wheeler, trailer in tow. She got on the I-15 freeway near Victorville, taking it all the way to the Rift. She pulled into the Freeway Viewpoint, and then followed the signs to the West Rim Trailhead. This was her first choice to get Arcon across the Rift. But her dad was right. There was no way to explain to Arcon how to find it from his side.

She drove back to the broken freeway section. A wall of concrete barriers blocked access to the edge of the cliff. Arcon could easily find this location, and the Rift was only half as wide here. She looked around the area. *No way we'll do this without being seen.*

She left the viewpoint and made her way up the often-patched road past the tourist town of Calico. Many still called it Calico Ghost Town, but it wasn't.

When the Rift opened in the early twenty-first century, the hills surrounding Calico became dotted with "earthquake-proof cabins," so people could experience the quakes, and, if lucky, watch a section of the escarpment slide into the abyss. No one cared about the silver mining history of the town, or how the earthquakes almost completely destroyed its historical buildings.

Elaina had reserved the cabin that overlooked the Rift damaged section of the I-15 freeway. With a high-powered telescope she'd be able to see the point where Arcon was due to arrive at noon on Saturday.

Her dad's plan was to airlift food and a communication earpiece to him. Then they'd work to get him climbing gear to cross the Rift. The drone could haul a hundred pounds of equipment, but not a human. It could also help map Arcon's route and follow his progress.

Rescuing people was something she did nearly every week, but none of those operations were done in secret. Most were performed under the command of authorities, such as county sheriffs or park rangers. Here, she was planning the details of the rescue, and the authorities were being kept in the dark.

She had no choice. The Mojave Forest was restricted to human intrusion. People weren't to hike, drive, or even fly over it. If God wanted her to do this, she must avoid the risk of others interfering. She put her faith in God working out the details.

Elaina had entered a restricted area before, rescuing someone who had disobeyed the rules and gotten lost. But that place was designated a wild area, set aside by Jesus to give the land and its animals rest from human activity. In that case, the rescue was authorized because proper order was being restored.

The Mojave Forest was restricted, period. There was no explanation given why, and no exceptions to the rule. Only Jesus could countermand the restriction. In her heart, Elaina believed she had received His permission. She hadn't gone through the human chain of command to obtain it. She'd gone straight to the top. She didn't want human authorities involved until it was over.

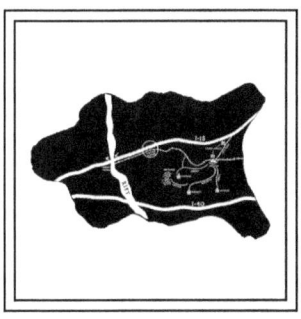

CHAPTER THIRTEEN

The hunters huddled in one of the few open areas of the forest. One by one Danner asked them their thoughts on how Arcon was traveling. They shrugged their shoulders.

Chad said, "I don't see how we'll catch him." He showed the blood spots on his arms. Sander agreed.

Danner scanned the group. "Did any of you notice a pattern with his movements? Come on, think about it."

Chad said, "He sure seems to zig and zag a lot."

They were quiet for a bit, looking around the forest, as if trying to get their bearings. "I don't know if it means anything," said Tawny, "but he seems to be going west, not south."

"Precisely," said Danner. "I think it's time for Derik to initiate Plan B." He let out a strange series of whistles. The others looked at him in confusion. "Well, boys, it's time to head back." Just then they heard a distant whistle from Derik calling them back to the Sunset Outpost. Danner just smiled and led them that direction.

An odd three-part whistle pierced the forest. Arcon sensed it was far in the distance. The first whistle had just been to get someone's attention. The next had identified the whistler as Danner. But the last one troubled him. He'd never heard it before. *Danner must be communicating something to Derik that they concocted for this occasion.*

The whistle that followed he was certain of; Derik was calling off the search. That would be welcome news if he knew what Danner's whistle meant. Arcon decided to stay put and wait. He needed the rest, and he desperately needed to eat.

He picked a handful of rhizome berries from the needle brush, but he knew he could only eat a few without protein to balance. There were certain digestion issues he really didn't need at the moment. He reluctantly ate a piece of goat jerky from his pack and had a swallow of water from a canteen. Then he lay back and stared up at all the tempting fruit on the ArcPoint trees.

His plan had been to eat that fruit all along, so he'd carried none in his pack. He'd already eaten more of his jerky than he should have. He'd have to wait until dusk to gather fruit, since it grew high enough to make him visible.

When his strength returned, he headed west, being careful to stay below the ridge top. Before long, he came to a steep rocky slope that blocked his path. It looked too steep to climb, and it continued south as far as he could see. This obstacle was not in his plans and not on his map. He didn't have time to go around it, so he reversed and started climbing back up to the top of Far Ridge, gambling that Derik was no longer searching for him.

Thankfully, the hills here were barren. He scampered over the rocks to make up some time, but climbing up through the crevices was a challenge. His moccasins were better suited for tree branches. He jumped to one rock for a better route up, and his foot slipped on the loose sandstone. His body slid into a crevice, where his right foot twisted and got wedged. Pain shot up his leg when he tried to pull free.

Without thinking, he almost cut loose with the most serious of all whistles, one that meant 'hunter in trouble.' Panic raced through him as he considered his situation. If he whistled or cried out to the hunters, they may not even hear him, and if they did, his journey was over. He would never see Elaina, and the Community may never let him use the transmitter to contact her. He had to calm down and free his foot. He had to pray.

Father, thank you for helping me get this far. Please forgive my impatience and grant me some understanding. I need insight on how to free my foot safely, and I need your healing touch so I can continue. And please, Lord, don't let it be broken. I need to get to Elaina, as I believe you want me to. I leave the solution to you, but I need to get moving.

Arcon tugged lightly again on his leg, and the pain was severe. Looking close, he could see a small bump of rock by his ankle that was blocking his foot from pulling free. It was painful, but he twisted around to where he could grab the heel of his moccasin. With a quick tug he pulled straight back on the moccasin and his foot slid out of the crevice. He tried rotating his foot. It was painful, but didn't appear to be broken. *Thank you, Lord.*

He gimped his way to the top of the ridge. On the other side, he could see his original goal. The map marked it as the Wilhelm Wash, a low spot between the north and south portions of Far Ridge. It was partially visible from the Sunset Outpost, but the ridge still hid his location south of it.

With dusk approaching, he had a decision to make. He was now a full day behind schedule and wanted to make up some time. But wisdom—and his ankle—were telling him to stop and rest. Give the hunters one more night to give up and move out.

He hiked toward the wash for another hour, while the hills still hid his progress. Then he spotted a clearing with a level spot clear of needle brush. It probably had rock close to the surface that kept the rhizomes from taking root. He'd camp there tonight and make a mad dash through the low spot in the morning.

◆

Elaina positioned the tripod in front of the window. She stole glances at the view while mounting the high-powered telescope. She tightened down the retainer. From this room she could see Rift Falls, the old freeway, and the Mojave Forest. The predominant feature by far was the Rift itself, stretching as far as she could see in both directions.

As Elaina attached the digital camera to the telescope, her shoulder phone squawked. She answered, "Hi Dad".

"Hi girl, are you in the room?"

"Yep. Just setting up the telescope."

"How's it look?"

"The telescope?"

"Very funny."

"There's a panoramic view. I can see why this room commands the extra credits. I see quite a ways down the old freeway."

"Great, that's perfect. Hey, it looks like I'll be on call this Saturday."

"Daaaad!"

"I know, I know. But I'll still drive there on Friday and bring the roll up big screen. We'll just have to pray I don't get called."

"Well, okay, as long as I get the big screen."

"Oh, I get it. I'm not needed. Maybe I'll send the screen to you in a driverless taxi. "

"And miss seeing my smiling face? You'd never do that."

"True. I'll see you Friday. In the morning if I can."

"See you then. Call me early tomorrow?"

"Of course. Big D out."

"Girl out."

Arcon gathered wood and readied a fire, with extra limbs piled nearby. It was still light, with a clear sky. He reached in his pack and pulled out his Grandpa Lee's journal.

He opened it in the middle, wanting to enjoy the parts his grandma read most often. These were the pages the ArcPoint Faithful read from to convince everyone not to leave the forest.

> *Took my daily walk around the Facility again. I'm still amazed at what God has accomplished in this place. I know of nowhere in the world where his peace is this pervasive.*
>
> *How could I have possibly brought together such an accomplished group of people? It seems every time we have a need, someone has the know-how, and someone else has the tools. Who in this day and age collects blacksmith hammers? Who stockpiles seed packets, food canners, and sardines? Who in their right mind goes on a camp-out in the desert with ten apple boxes full of DIY books?*
>
> *Descendants of Noah may have thought he was a gifted zoologist. But it was God who brought in the animals, just as he gathered the right people to this desert. Then he brought us the rains that others didn't expect. We have an abundance of food, and thankfully not as much rain as Noah got.*
>
> *We just built a room full of things from the past to remember the way it was in the outside world. I don't think I want to remember. In fact, I appreciate the days God allows me to forget.*

Arcon didn't want to forget ArcPoint, but he had to forsake it. He was glad he'd brought the journal. He would remember.

He recognized the next entry. It had been difficult for his grandma to read it aloud, so he'd heard it only a few times. It told about when Grandpa Lee's wife died. Arcon's grandma was only related by marriage, but she'd always referred to Victoria as Grandma.

> *Buried my best friend this week. She was suffering at the end, so I'm sure it was a blessing for her to be done with that. Now I have to learn to live without her.*

I can't complain. Almost lost her thirty years ago. So, at nearly a hundred years old, God allowed me to enjoy her longer than I expected. Would have loved her company a few more years if I could have though.

She'd probably want me to write down more of my feelings, but I just don't feel like it. I have to admit though; if it weren't for her, I wouldn't be writing anything at all. I'd be dead, and this place probably wouldn't exist.

Time to take my walk.

Arcon didn't know if he would ever see the ArcPoint community again. But if he did, he would take a walk around it like Grandpa Lee had. If things worked out, maybe Elaina would walk at his side. But that would be later. First, he wanted to experience every form of travel that still existed. He wanted to see the natural wonders of God's creation. And he wanted someone to share those discoveries with.

Elaina seemed like the type of person who would enjoy such a life. He didn't know a lot about her, but he'd pieced together an image. She traveled around to rescue people, so she was adventurous. She didn't care to cook, which meant she spent her time outside the home. She'd found him, which meant she was a diligent searcher. Most importantly, she was convinced God wanted them together. There had to be a reason for that.

He and Brina were different in a lot of ways. Her family was thriving. His had died off. Her descendant brought life to the ArcPoint Community, versatile plants bred to grow larger every day. His descendant built structures, all of which were deteriorating. And Brina had no desire to climb a tree.

He put the journal back in his pack and pulled out the goat hide. In his apartment it was a rug, but on this journey it was a blanket, and his map. On the underside he'd drawn out where he would go to get to the I-15 freeway. As he looked it over, he realized he was entering land he knew nothing about.

Some of what he'd drawn was from maps so old they didn't even have the Rift on them. He'd drawn that feature from other descriptions. His map was detailed in areas he'd personally been to. But all of that ended at Far Ridge. It'd surely changed a lot since Jarden was here as a young man.

Black crayon followed a line that ran diagonally to the middle left side. This was his goal, the I-15. A red line ran horizontally through the middle of ArcPoint until it met with the black line. That was the railroad tracks.

Jarden had told him the Union Pacific Company dug up the track when the Rift happened. They used the materials to build a new connecting line somewhere to the east. The only track left went through ArcPoint property and was overgrown.

A blue line below marked the ArcPoint River, or what the ancient maps called the Mojave River. Where Arcon was headed, all three lines were near each other. The trees loved the river and would be large there. Their seeds were carried toward the Rift by birds and squirrels into the low land that was once the Mojave River.

If he could make it to those big trees, there would be sturdy branches to run on. But doing that was often like trying to solve a maze. You could run a series of branches only to reach a dead end and have to backtrack.

If he continued west, the trees occurred in patches from seeds planted by ground squirrels. Most had branches too small to run on, but unfortunately did a good job of creating thorny rhizomes.

The needle-brush grew thick in the gravel of the old railroad. He'd have to cross through it to get to the I-15. Between that and his bad ankle, he didn't think he'd make the rendezvous point in time. He saw no other choice.

He lit the fire and coaxed the flames high. He laid down on the leaves he'd gathered for bedding and threw the hide over himself. Tomorrow he could concentrate on making the journey and surviving it.

CHAPTER FOURTEEN

FRIDAY

When daylight broke, Arcon rolled onto his back and stretched. He pulled the goat hide over his shoulders for a little more warmth before getting up. He stared at a pinkish blue sky that would soon alter the chill he now felt. His natural temptation to stay covered was broken by the sight of fruit in the trees. He remembered where he was. Both excitement and hunger brought him to his feet. His ankle ached, but he could now put weight on it. He tested it with a careful climb to get fruit.

The dew trap had done its job well, thanks to the cold. He'd need more for the next few days. He could always get more fluids from the tree fruit.

Securing his machete scabbard to his back, he hiked north, zigzagging through the open areas in the berry vines. With no trees or rhizomes, he rarely needed to hack at vines, and his arms thanked him for that. But his nose and ears didn't appreciate the sunlight. Even his long hair was letting through more light than was comfortable. He wanted to cover his head, but the poncho with the hood was too warm to wear.

He continued north toward some tall trees he'd spotted. From their height he could plot his course, and there would be shadows to hide in, although he believed the hunters had given up. To stay closer to the Rift, he wanted to head northwest—

not north—to locate the old I-15 freeway. All the elders were convinced the I-15 was buried under needle brush.

Arcon had a theory. Even if the trees covered the road, the road was there. The trees could not get a taproot down to the aquifer like the others could. That meant they should be small and sparse.

It wasn't yet straight up sun but curiosity trumped caution, prompting Arcon to climb the tree near the top of the hill. What he saw from the top branches frightened him. The Rift. He'd no idea it was so large, so expansive. If it were as deep as it was wide, he would be in trouble. He could only hope Elaina could get him across.

Below him was a small creek flowing due west toward the Rift. That was not right. The creek in the Wilhelm Wash flowed north. He wasn't where he wanted to be. To his right he saw Far Ridge, so the ridge he'd been following was wrong. As near as he could tell, he was twice as far from the ArcPoint River as he needed to be.

Arcon could see patches of ArcPoint trees all the way to the Rift, and needle brush surrounded it all. Forest patches would make the I-15 even harder to locate. *Where is that auto-path, anyway?*

He turned his back to the sun. The I-15 should hit the Rift in front of him and to the left. He scanned for any sign of an unfamiliar patch of color, but saw none. It all appeared to be groves of trees, needle brush, or grass and other vegetation. There was another small hill in front of him with tall trees on it. He'd head there next to get a different view.

Jarden kept as still as he could near the top of the elder ArcPoint tree. He'd trained Arcon extensively on how to use bunny bird hawks to locate rabbits and discern movement in the forest, including human. If he wasn't careful, the birds would spot Jarden, and so would Arcon. He slowly brought the nocs to his eyes.

He was about to lower them when he saw movement in the trees. It was slight, but it was someplace to look. He focused the nocs for that distance and… strike. Even in shadow he could identify Arcon's lithe body.

Arcon appeared to be studying his surroundings, probably planning his route. *Keep heading northwest, young man, keep heading northwest.* He was pleased he'd been correct regarding Arcon's plans, but it also troubled him. Arcon was headed for the Rift.

As a young boy, Jarden had stood on the edge of that canyon. Far below was the bony carcass of a large animal, probably driven over the side by wolves. How his heart had ached for that poor animal's life and its manner of death.

Jarden's dad explained that it was the way of the world, what he described as survival of the fittest. God said someday the lion would lie down with the lamb, the coyote and rabbit would play together. Maybe they'd live to see it.

What Jarden had to shake from his mind was that carcass. He'd always associated the Rift with death, and couldn't bear the thought of Arcon at the bottom of that canyon. He wanted to believe Arcon had a plan, that he wouldn't try it without God's guidance.

There could be no peace in his life until he caught up to Arcon. He needed to challenge Arcon to reveal his plan, or persuade him to abandon the journey. If God gave Arcon a vision, Jarden needed to know.

He waited until Arcon climbed down, then did the same.

Elaina followed the Rift trail south for a couple kilometers, stopping occasionally to peer over the edge to scan the eastern side, disobeying the warning signs. She only knew Arcon would approach the I-15 from the south, but not how close he would be to the Rift when he did so.

As she stared at the wall of rock across the canyon, it looked different from what she remembered. There used to be a precarious bunch of rock jutting out of the face of the cliff where she'd stood as a fourteen-year-old girl. Time had changed the Rift, and it had changed her as well. She was no longer the teenager begging her dad to let her find the Morse code stranger.

Many times their conversation had stopped for long periods, either from technical issues or because her father insisted she stop. But somehow she and Arcon always reconnected, and the subject was often the same. He wanted out of that place and needed help to accomplish his escape.

At first he just wanted to see what was outside the forest he lived in. Then he talked of wanting to ride a bicycle, drive an auto, and fly in an airplane. She didn't have the heart to tell him almost nobody flew in airplanes anymore. Fuel was too scarce and land based travel was safer and nearly as fast.

Over the last year his desires had shifted from escaping, to a desire to be where she was. She hoped to find out soon what he meant by that.

He'd cautioned her to keep knowledge of him a secret, and she'd told no one. Except her father, of course. And her two best friends. And their friends. She actually had quite a few people encouraging her and praying for Arcon.

They all knew the stories about the Mojave cult and their fear of mankind. They also knew of the rumors of evil in that place. But Elaina had cautioned them not to pre-judge Arcon, or allow anyone else to.

She couldn't wait to really *talk* to Arcon—not tap messages to him in some code. She turned and looked at the trailer mounted on the back of her three-wheeler. She was tempted to unload the drone right now and fly it across the Rift to search for him. Instead, she stared at the crumbling cliff wall of the Rift. This would not be an easy climb for Arcon.

CHAPTER FIFTEEN

As Noreena Chan started down the Rift trail, she spotted a young Hispanic girl staring at the canyon wall. Curious about people's lives, she asked, "Did you have family close to here when this happened?"

Startled by this stranger, Elaina answered, "Too close."

"I don't mean to pry, but did you lose someone?"

"My great-grandparents, who lived in Daggett. The building they lived in collapsed on them. My grandfather was only three at the time. He was trapped in the rubble for two days."

"Your grandfather was alive when the quake hit?" asked Noreena. "That was a long time ago. Do you mean your great-grandfather?"

Elaina smiled. "No, it was my grandfather. He was eighty years old when my father was born. Over a hundred when he died. If he hadn't survived the earthquake, I wouldn't be talking to you right now."

"I'm sorry for your loss."

"Did you—lose someone, I mean?"

"No, not in this earthquake. But this was one of the first major quakes that spared us."

"What do you mean?"

"Did you ever hear of the Tangshan earthquake?"

Elaina shook her head. "No, I don't think so."

"It killed over a quarter million people in China in 1976. Some were family on my dad's side."

"Wow. I'm surprised I never heard of it."

"Most people here haven't. But that's not all. My surviving relatives lived in Hong Kong and moved to Japan in the late 1990s. Many of them died in a tsunami that hit in 2011, also caused by a quake. Those who survived moved to a Chinese community in Vancouver, Canada. But that area started experiencing many small quakes; what they called a slow slip. It made them nervous, so they moved to Portland, Oregon."

"Oh, no," said Elaina as she put her hand to her mouth. "Don't tell me…"

"Yes, they were living in downtown Portland when it collapsed. Many survived, but were devastated by what they experienced."

"How terrible."

"Yes, it was. But God turned it into good."

"Really?"

"My family were practicing Buddhists and were helped after the quake by members of a Mandarin and English church. They learned about the Creator of all mankind and how to hear his voice. In faith, they asked God where they should flee from the earthquakes. He told them to stay in Portland and rebuild. It would be shook no more."

"And it hasn't, has it?"

"Portland never again had a serious quake. Not even aftershocks."

"This area shook for over two years as the Rift expanded. Much of California did. My grandpa was taken in by one of the men who dug him out of the rubble. He and his wife raised Grandpa with a belief in God, and eventually to rescue people as well."

"So, is that what he did for a living?" asked Noreena.

"No, he went to school and became a male nurse, then a paramedic. But he often volunteered with search and rescue teams, and his medical skills helped."

"So, did he marry another medical professional, or someone he rescued?"

"He married a nurse at … wait a minute. I never said he got married."

Noreena smiled. "If he hadn't, I wouldn't be talking with you. Right?"

Elaina laughed and said, "Oh, yeah, good catch. You must be a detective."

"Not at all," said Noreena. "A reporter."

"Uh-oh, that reminds me. I was supposed to report in to my dad. Nice to meet you. Gotta go."

Noreena watched the young girl dart away toward the parking lot. Something about the encounter hadn't seemed right.

She shook it off as reporter instincts run amok. But she'd gotten some of her best stories by stepping into someone else's private life. She made mental notes of the girl's face. They both drove the same brand of three-wheeled autocycle, but this girl's had a unique trailer. She'd keep an eye out for it, just in case. She wished they had exchanged names.

Elaina hadn't meant to be rude, but the last person in the world she wanted to talk with was a reporter. Even a detective or judge would have been better. They questioned people in private. A reporter would broadcast the news to everyone possible, leaving the truth to go adrift in a sea of words.

Her dad had gone before judges many times, following rescue missions. Truth was the goal of judges, and she believed the truth about the Mojave People needed to be told. She just wanted to hear it from Arcon first.

Her plan was to sneak Arcon across the Rift and get him home without publicity. He'd stay in the basement, and her dad would help her question him about the Mojave People. Elaina was sure they wouldn't need the locks her dad had installed on the basement door.

◆

Arcon wished the pesky bunny birds would go away. He wasn't as concerned about them revealing his location, but didn't want to take any chances. He'd hide for a while, and they'd dissipate. But not long after he started moving they were back. They would be flying in a big circle, then see him and fly a tight circle directly overhead, and then leave. Classic behavior when encountering a human that was scaring all of the rodents into the ground.

The sun approached straight up. His face was hot, even in the shade, and he was dead tired. His ankle wasn't slowing him down much, but it was complaining.

He found a nicely curved tree trunk in the shade and grabbed his next-to-last piece of goat jerky. He nestled against the tree with his Grandpa Lee's journal. He was curious if there were other things his grandma had screened from him. He scanned the early journal for mention of the trees. On page sixteen he found:

> Got a visit from some political activists today. Mike called them enviro-mentals. They're worried about all the tiny houses and construction going on. Afraid too many people are encroaching near the wilderness. Seems we can't find peace anywhere. They even got a lawyer. That's the last thing I want to deal with.
>
> One of them found out the RED-C used to do genetic modification with plants. We assured them we don't have any genetic research lab. We're simply trying to develop trees for biofuel. Thankfully, they liked that we were trying to reduce the need for fossil fuels. I hope that's the last we see of them.

Arcon didn't know who Mike was, but he remembered RED-C was the company the Facility came from—the Renewable Energy Development Consortium. It was the common link between the Founders, who'd either worked for the RED-C or for his Grandpa Lee when he built their facility.

He knew something had gone wrong. The trees didn't grow as expected, and that's why the ArcPoint Community got separated from the rest of mankind. *Grandma believed God did it for our own good, but what did Grandpa Lee have to say about it?*

Assuming there had to be something from Grandpa Lee in the journal, he started looking for some reference to it. Halfway through he found:

> *Norm came in all freaked out today. Took me over to the plantings by the riverbed. The trees are growing gonzo out there, now that steady rain has the river flowing. I didn't see a problem until he showed me some thorny vines growing out from the base of the trees. He called them rhizomes. Never seen such a thing. Wicked thorns on them. Emphasize wicked.*
>
> *Norm's convinced it's something the RED-C did to the rootstock before we got them. He confessed knowing about the genetic experimentation and apologized for not telling me. He wants to study them and experiment a bit. The berries growing on them may be edible.*
>
> *I can tell he's rattled. There's something he's not telling me.*

Arcon's heart leapt. There had to be more to the story. Several pages later he found the entry:

> *We've reached the breaking point with the rhizomes. We should have wiped them out. The goats can't eat the shoots fast enough. Nothing seems to kill them, and everyone is worn out from trying to chop them back or dig them up. They're like weeds. If you leave any roots, you get another tree.*
>
> *There are a few good things though. The berries are edible. The rhizomes produce a tree with seeds we can use as flour. That's huge. Seeds from the berries produce*

a blackberry that's real tasty. But the vines have wicked thorns. We're hoping the good outweighs the bad.

Consensus is, we concentrate our efforts on where we live. Set up a perimeter beyond which we just let the plants do their thing. We'll keep a few paths open through that barrier, but otherwise we just keep our own space clear. Let the vines grow into a wall. Besides, it'll help to keep outsiders out and the coyotes away from the chickens. Without heavy equipment to eradicate them, that's what it will have to be. God help us.

Arcon had always assumed growing the vines was intentional. The old-timers touted the berries and the seeds as being a God given blessing. He agreed with Grandpa Lee that the thorns were a curse, but without the seeds to make flour they wouldn't have noodles. He hoped the outside world could make spaghetti without having to deal with thorns.

He put the journal away. Now he felt better about sacrificing himself to investigate what was outside the wall. The Community was losing resources that couldn't be replaced. Only twelve varieties of fruits and vegetables have survived, after starting with thirty. Every generator had failed except one.

Brina was another example of what the Community had lost. Women rarely gave birth to girls. They thought they'd figured out the cause, but the condition was worse. He hoped the outside world had a cure. He pictured how upset Brina would be. He should have at least left her a note.

He was in unfamiliar territory, not only in the forest, but in life as well. *Father, your word says if I choose my way, you will direct my steps. Open my eyes to see the best path, my heart to choose the right helper. Please protect me through it all. Thanks.*

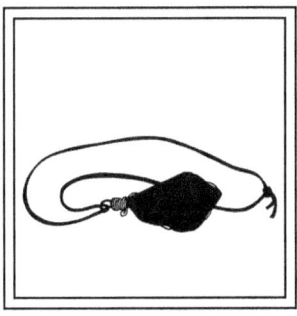

CHAPTER SIXTEEN

The water in his canteen was lower than expected, and in the sun he needed more. If he didn't find a water source, he'd need to climb more often for fruit. *What day is this?* He counted and realized it was Friday. He needed to get to the rendezvous point by Saturday. He'd have to hurry.

The sun bore down on him, even though it was early morning. He was closing in on more trees and hacked furiously to reach their shade. He thought he heard something. He stopped, listened, and looked around, but couldn't see anything. He went back to hacking.

Later, while walking along a tree branch, a man stepped out from behind its trunk. Arcon was so startled, he jerked away and nearly fell.

"Be careful, Arcon," said Jarden. "You're a long way from the Med shack."

Arcon stared in disbelief at the gray-haired man in front of him. At eighty years old Jarden Merrick was still strong, with a needle sharp mind. He'd been a hunter for over fifty years. Obviously he'd not lost his skills.

"I'm here to take you home, son."

"How … Where did you … How did you find me?"

Jarden chuckled. "When Derik first spotted you running, I realized you were farther west than any of us expected. I took a chance you were headed for the I-15 and tried to get north of you. I had Bill Winters go silently around to the west."

"You *flanked* me?" asked Arcon. "With Bill? He never would've caught me."

"We only needed his eyes and his whistle. Besides, he had Sander with him. We figured you were trying to fool us, but weren't sure if your new swingway was part of the plan or part of the trick."

"How did you figure out I was trying to leave? I might have just gone to work on my swingway or something."

Jarden looked him in the eyes. "I found something missing."

Arcon's eyes got big. "You're mad I took Grandpa's journal?"

"You did what?" Jarden asked. "Lee Franklin's journal? No, no, that's yours anyway. I was talking about the rock in your room. The one you polished for your grandmother."

"The one you gave me? Why did that tip you off?"

"You'd never carry it if you meant to return."

Arcon's chin began to quiver. He looked away. "I wanted something to remember her by, and it was the only thing small enough to carry." He was silent for a moment. "And I wanted to remember you."

"Thank you, son. It's an honor to be on a level with her. Did you know I found the rough rock close to here?"

"You did?" said Arcon, his voice going up an octave. "Where?"

"Just over that ridge, on the side of a hill, before the trees and needle-brush reached this area."

Arcon looked around at all the vegetation, then turned back to Jarden. "I still don't know how you found me in all of this."

"I saw you up in the tree yesterday, and under one a few minutes ago, and I watched the bunny birds. I just let you come to me."

"But how did you know I'd take this route?"

"Arcon, I've known you your whole life, and I paid attention," said Jarden, grinning. "For some reason you never had a fear of the Rift. Myself, I've seen it, and I'd have headed south till I was well past it." He paused. "I know you're trying to go see the outsider gal you've been communicating with."

"Her name is Elaina."

"Okay, I know you're trying to get to Elaina. I figured she must be involved in helping you get across somehow. The easiest place for outsiders would be where the road stabilizes the cliff walls. If you do this, outsiders will know about us. Have you given any thought to what will happen to ArcPoint when they do?"

That was the one thing Arcon tried *not* to think about. He looked at the branch he was standing on and saw a fork in it. Perfect for sitting on. "We might as well stay awhile," he said, gesturing toward the trunk of the tree. "I know you won't let this go until we've talked it through."

"I was hoping you'd say that," said Jarden. He pulled the short machete scabbard from behind him, rested it on his lap, and leaned back, trying a few positions until he was comfortable. Then he slid the machete out of its scabbard and stabbed the point into the tree branch. "That's better," he said, using the machete handle as an armrest.

"You understand I *have* thought this through," said Arcon. "Over there, Elaina has the same problem. She could be in a lot of trouble for helping me. But we're both convinced God is asking us to do what we're doing. We believe everything will work out, somehow." Arcon went silent and turned his face away.

"What is it, son?"

Arcon glared back at him. "You're forcing me to rethink everything. If God wanted me to get through, why would he guide you to where I was? Or did you just pick this place by chance?"

"I knew if you ever tried it, you'd take the only other sensible route for tree-walkers like us." Jarden hung his head. "I do believe God guided me to you."

"To try and stop me? How do you plan to do that?"

Jarden noticed Arcon staring at the machete. Jarden jerked it out of the branch and got to his feet. "I respect your drive, your honesty. I even understand your concerns about the Community.

But a hunter should never go it alone, like you're doing" Holding the machete, he extended his arm. "A wounded hunter can't make it out alive." He dropped the machete to the ground.

Arcon watched it fall through the needle brush and land point first in the forest floor. He looked his mentor squarely in the eyes. "How do you plan on getting that back?"

Jarden looked down at the machete, which was still wiggling. "Good question. If you're not going back with me, I'll need it. Care to give me a hand?"

Arcon felt a wave of relief sweep over him. "You never really planned to stop me, did you?"

Jarden shook his head. "For the sake of the Community I had to try, or at least say I did. But I was pretty convinced I wouldn't have the will to try hard enough."

"Then why come out here?"

"To be honest, son, I was concerned I'd never see you again. If you have to leave, I want you to be successful wherever God leads you. But I needed to know if it was really God leading you, and not just a passion for adventure, or a wife."

Arcon stared into the forest. "Probably all of those. I do want to see what's outside this forest, and I'd like to have a wife to share it with. But do you remember the story in the Bible about Paul going to Jerusalem? God called him to do it, but also prepared him for the dangers. It's the same with me. I can't explain it, but I have to do this."

"That's what I needed to hear," said Jarden. "I'd like to pray with you, that God gives you peace and protects you."

Arcon approached the short stocky man, put one hand on the tree trunk, and threw the other arm around him. "Thanks, boss," he said as they hugged. "I really need that."

"Before I do, let me give you the best advice you're likely to get on this crazy adventure of yours."

"What's that?" asked Arcon.

"See this tree? Climb it as high as you can. I'll be right behind you."

Arcon started climbing and soon discovered that the tree was one of the tallest in the area. When he'd gone as high as he could, he looked down at Jarden and said, "I think this is about it."

"Good," said Jarden, "That should be high enough." Then he removed the binoculars from around his neck and handed them to Arcon. "Tell me what you see on the horizon."

Arcon looked around, scanning to different places. "For one thing, I don't see any ArcPoint trees beyond the Rift."

Jarden laughed. "That's probably good for everyone. What do you see at the very top edge of the horizon? Look west."

"I don't see anything—I mean, nothing in particular."

"Keep watching."

Arcon scanned the horizon. "Okay, I see something to the west. It looks like a bright spot. Oh, and there's another. And two more to the north of those."

"That's good," said Jarden. "I didn't know if we could see them. Let me look." Jarden took the nocs. "My dad told me about this when I was about your age. Well, look at that! There's over a dozen now."

"What are they, boss?" asked Arcon.

"You might call them the windows of Heaven. In reality, they're the windows of Calico, reflecting the sunlight. What a sight."

"That's Calico?" he asked. "I've seen it on the maps."

"The actual town is further west. They built cabins for the tourists with large windows facing the Rift. My dad saw this over a hundred years ago and never forgot it. Lucky for you I happened along."

"Why do you say that?"

"Didn't your girl tell you to go to our side of the I-15? It only makes sense she would. It's identifiable, and a stable part of the Rift. If she did, those cabins are the logical place she'd stay to watch for you. She's probably there right now."

"You're kidding."

Jarden handed back the nocs. "Head straight for that spot. Note the shape of the hills, because those lights won't always be there. You'll reach the I-15 and the Rift before Calico."

Arcon stared at the lights and scanned the surrounding hills while he had the nocs. He looked down at Jarden. "How can I ever thank you?"

"Go to her, son. Find that gal and take her for a life partner if it works out—and I pray it will. Have kids if you can. If you have a son, name him Jarden and we'll be even."

"I agree to your terms." Arcon shook his hand and gave him back the binoculars. Then he looked around, back toward Calico, and back at Jarden. "Can you join me?"

"You know I can't. The Community needs me. And though many will disagree, they need you to help us connect with the world again. I don't believe it's as bad out there as it used to be, but no one really knows, unless Elaina told you something."

"No, we couldn't converse. But I heard enough to trust she's a true believer. Maybe evil still exists. I don't know anything for sure."

"But you learned enough to get both of us up this tree," said Jarden, laughing. They climbed down until they were on a large branch closest to the ground.

Arcon asked, "Could you do one thing for me before you leave?"

"Sure, what's that?"

"Could you look at my map?"

"You have a map?" Jarden asked.

"Sort of," responded Arcon. "Let me show you." He pulled the rolled up goatskin from his pack and spread it out over the trunk of the tree. "If I'm correct, we should be somewhere in this area."

"This is the rug from your apartment, isn't it?"

Arcon smiled. "Sometimes it's best to hide things in plain sight. Plus, it keeps me warm at night."

"Smart move. Where'd you find colored markers?"

"In the Room of Remembrance. Don't worry, I put them back. Besides, they were mine anyway. Grandma Franklin put them in there."

Jarden looked at an unmarked green line. "Is this your swingway?"

"Yeah. I ran out of time to take it beyond Far Ridge though. I thought I could sneak past Derik."

"Nothing gets past Derik."

"I found that out." Arcon looked him in the eye. "I'm sorry about lying to you."

"I can see why you felt you had to," said Jarden. "But no more, understand?"

"Perfectly," said Arcon. "See anything else?"

"The windows of Calico are right about here," said Jarden, pointing to the left side of the map. "Now, down here is an area you may want to visit. Several houses were in this area before the Rift happened. Then they were abandoned. Some of us used to pilfer building materials from there."

"How'd you do that?"

"You know the old tractor parked by the Griffin place?"

"Really? That was still running then?"

"Oh yeah. Life was a lot easier when we had that thing working. We'd go down to those houses with a trailer and haul stuff home. That's why I know how bad it would be to go south. The earth cracks just kept going, sometimes on both sides of us. Anyway, if you can't cross the Rift, you may be able to find shelter there."

"Thanks. Good to know."

"I see you marked the railroad tracks. And this circle says, *cross here?*"

"That should be the best spot to get to the I-15," said Arcon.

"I'm not so sure about that. The railroad followed the river, and you know what that means."

"It's a jungle," responded Arcon, sounding worried.

"That's right. No one in their right mind would try to cross it."

"To be honest, I've had second thoughts myself," confessed Arcon. "Elaina is supposed to have some way to talk with me and help guide my way, but I must get closer to the Rift. I'll make my decision after I talk with her."

Jarden just shook his head. "I don't like it, son. I hope she has a solid plan. I'll pray for you." Arcon nodded.

Jarden put one arm around him and raised one to the sky. *"Father, this son of yours has a mission—a tough one. You've got a daughter on the other side in the same way. I ask you to lead them to each other and keep them safe. Open their eyes to the best path, their minds to hear your Spirit."*

"And help Jarden find a path back home with good branches and sparse needle-brush," added Arcon.

"Amen to that, son. *And amen to you, Father."* Jarden turned and gave Arcon a hug. "I'll want to see you again, and your lady friend, too. Always keep that in mind."

"I'll never forget you, boss."

"The name is Jarden, son. Don't forget that. Don't go naming your son Boss," he joked, smacking Arcon on the shoulder. "Before you go, I've got something I want you to have." Jarden reached inside the collar of his goat hair sweater. He pulled out something attached to a leather string that was around his neck.

"What is it?"

Jarden handed it to him. "It's a pendant I made."

Arcon looked it over. "It's a beautiful stone. You did a nice job on the wire wrapping too. Or did someone else do that?"

"I did it all."

Arcon looked closer. "Is that copper from car wiring?"

"Mainly. The binding is from an old motor."

"You made this for me?"

Jarden's face contorted as he looked toward the ground. "No."

"What do you mean?"

"I made it ..." Jarden's chin quivered as he looked at Arcon. "I made it for Sasha, your mother." He looked into the expanse of the forest. "I never got the chance to give it to her."

They both fell silent. Even the forest seemed to grow quiet at that moment. Arcon spoke first. "You need to keep it yourself, and share it with the Community."

"Son, this is going around your neck. If it goes back to the Community, so are you. I know it hurts to remember how your parents died, but it was an accident. We both need to let go of the guilt we share."

"But I was the one who was disobedient."

"And I encouraged that disobedience. Arcon, what Zoreb and Sasha experienced at the moment that lab exploded was the greatest joy us humans can encounter. They felt no pain. Our medical people confirmed that. They were instantly with Jesus in Paradise."

Arcon looked him in the eyes. "But how could God allow such a thing to happen?"

"I don't mean to state the obvious, but, He must have loved them more than we did."

"I know, you're right."

"Tell you what. We'll see them again some day, and when we do, hand that pendant back to me so I can give it to your mother."

Arcon stared at him, one eyebrow raised. Then he smiled. "I agree to your terms."

" Great, now get moving. Be good. And if not, don't let God see you."

Arcon chuckled as he climbed down to retrieve Jarden's machete.

"He's yours now, Lord," said Jarden under his breath.

CHAPTER SEVENTEEN

There was an increased sense of urgency in Arcon's spirit, a renewed vigor in his limbs. The trees were getting shorter and sparser, but the lower branches were getting larger and farther off the ground. He had to jump higher for good branches, but so far he'd been able to do it. He climbed once more to look for an open area.

What he saw forced him to change his plans. This line of trees took him no closer to the I-15, but thankfully ended with very little needle-brush. Far beyond he could see buildings. Those had to be the ones Jarden told him about. Beyond those buildings was the Rift. He'd go there, spend the night, and then head north.

He tried to estimate how far he was from the I-15, but he couldn't see any sign of it. It was obvious the forest was immense at this point. To the north must be where the ArcPoint River met the Rift. The trees and needle-brush thrived there.

He could make out the hills where the windows of Calico were. They weren't visible from the ground, but if he could get smoke to rise high enough, maybe Elaina would see it. *Maybe there's something in those old buildings to make a fire with.* He'd burn one of them down if he had to.

Elaina stayed in her cabin most of the day on Friday, peering through the telescope and drinking coffee. Sadly, she had to do it without her dad and the roll-up screen. He said he'd probably arrive this evening, but things happen. She was half-hoping Arcon wouldn't show until tomorrow, as expected.

As she searched the trees, she recalled the history she'd read of the tribulation times when the Mojave People moved there. Lawlessness was profuse, even celebrated by some. Law enforcement abandoned large areas of cities and rural lands because of casualties and a lack of resources.

Fuel of every type was in short supply after oil refineries were damaged in the war. Fracking well casings broke in the quakes. Recreational travel halted, and personal vehicles rarely traveled great distances. With impassable roads, expensive fuel, and car thieves, residents stayed home. She wasn't surprised the Mojave People remained in hiding.

Around that time, earth's magnetic poles weakened and solar flare intensity peaked. The combination damaged the power grid. Satellites were disabled and fell from the sky over time. Central Authority never restarted a space program.

The people eventually funded a tube-train system that circled the country, making ground travel as fast as airplanes, and incredibly fuel-efficient. But that funding came at the expense of roads. Many highways remained impassable for decades. That was especially true for quake-damaged roads into the Mojave area.

A helicopter would be perfect for rescuing Arcon. But only the highest authorities could approve the use of any aircraft. It had to be a life or death situation, and this wasn't. This mission involved someone whom she could never receive approval for. *This is our only choice, Arcon. I'm ready when you are.*

Arcon tried the door of the abandoned house but it was locked. He walked around until he found a broken window, climbed through it, and walked back to the front door. He twisted the lock and pulled hard; the hinges crying as the rust in their joints gave way.

Most of the houses remaining in this once-upon-a-time neighborhood were wide open, showing evidence of a century of animal intruders. But with a good roof, locked doors, and most of the windows intact, even the birds had left this place alone. *This will make a good outpost, if I need one. It even has a fireplace.*

Fire. He'd planned to build a fire when he got to the I-15 to signal Elaina. *Why not here?* It was getting too dark, but he could gather wood and start a fire in the morning. *She probably has a star gazing telescope. She should be able to see a fire, even all the way from the windows of Calico.*

He wandered through the houses, picking up pieces of dry wood. He feared it wouldn't smoke much, and the fire needed to be identifiable as being from him. Rounding the corner, he saw an old truck. *I think those tires will burn, and the smoke will be black.* He grabbed his machete and chopped off some small pieces.

It took a while to get a good fire going with his flint, but soon it was producing a good column of smoke. He threw in a small piece of tire and watched it soften, then get glossy, and then ignite. He ran back outside and saw black smoke rising from the chimney. It dissipated a little and drifted to the east, but he believed it went higher than the trees.

He tried throwing a small chunk in the fire every so often, to see if he could produce something that looked like a dot or a dash. After several tries, he realized how futile his plan was. He wasn't even in the right location. He shrugged his shoulders. *She may not know where it's coming from, but she'll know it's me, even if it's not Morse code.*

Elaina kept her telescope focused on the area just above the waterfall. Wisps of fog were rolling up from the trees, which could be from the late-night air starting to cool. But some wisps were blackish. She couldn't imagine Arcon was lighting a signal fire this late in the day. If he were, he'd have to do better than that. It didn't surprise her that the signal was early, but it was difficult to discern, and in the wrong location.

She hoped he could get to the I-15 further east. The forest there looked sparse and narrow. With the bend the Rift took, she wouldn't be able to see past the trees until she was beyond the waterfall. *If that's him, he's on the wrong side of the forest.*

Land on that side of the Rift was at a higher elevation. She couldn't see the surface. To see Arcon on that side of the forest, he'd have to be on the very edge of the Rift. There wouldn't be clean, sturdy edges for him to stand on. No, for this to work he needed to be standing on the old freeway asphalt. It could take him another two days to traverse the forest. That may be out of the question.

Just then she heard a knock on the cabin door. She ran to the door, threw it open and yelled, "Dad, come look at this, I've seen something!"

She ran to the monitor. "What do you make of these black puffs of smoke? Ahhhrr, you were too slow. Just sit down and watch. They're coming every few minutes. WAIT! You have that big screen, right? Quick, let's get it set up before they go away. Come on!" She was out the door and headed to the Search and Rescue Vehicle before he could say a word.

Catching up to her, he pulled the roll-up monitor from the back seat. Elaina grabbed it from him and trotted back to the cabin.

"Hey girl, careful with that!" he yelled. "It only *looks* cheap."

In the cabin, Elaina rolled the monitor out on the tabletop. Roberto strode in carrying the cables. He carefully connected the screen to the laptop as Elaina scrambled to plug in the power cord.

"Sweeeet," said Elaina, when the screen came to life. "Okay, now—see this grove of trees right here? Remember how the waterfall spills out just below, about here? Okay, watch at the top of the trees right in this area and tell me if you see something different, something not, you know, *natural.*"

Her dad watched for a few minutes. Elaina twisted her hair with a forefinger. "*There!*" she said with excitement. "See that? What does that look like to you?"

He shrugged. "Looks like someone is burning garbage."

"Exactly—like burning plastic or rubber. Dad, that's coming from the other side of the Rift! I've hiked past that grove, and that can't be coming from this side. I think Arcon may be signaling me from beyond that grove of trees."

Roberto studied the black smoke as it slowly dissipated. "And it shows up every so often like that?"

"Yes. I've seen it three times now. There is a distinct pattern to it. Now, it's not Morse code like we agreed to. But I didn't think he could pull that off, anyway. This may be the best he can do."

Roberto backed the view out with the remote, then more. He looked around the area. He looked at the Rift, at the ends of the freeway, and focused in on the base of the trees. "If he's on the other side of the trees, that's not good, is it?"

Elaina shook her head. "No, it's not. The Rift is too wide and unstable where he is. And Dad, there are wolves in the woods."

"Do you mean coyotes?"

"I wish. It sounds like a small pack near the Rift. I think we need to contact him and get his input. He needs to know the dangers either way."

"Wolves aren't that dangerous, really, provided we respect their territory."

"But Dad, that's the restricted area. It could be a lot wilder over there."

"I agree. But remember, he's lived in that stuff his whole life. He's made it this far somehow." He looked around with the telescope, trying to find the spot they'd seen. "Girl, have you seen that black smoke again?"

"Are you in the right spot?"

"You tell me, but I think so."

Elaina stared at the screen, moved the telescope around a little, and crept back to where it had been. "That's the spot. I remember the waterfall was right where it is now. What do you think happened?"

"I don't know. Get on the searchnet and pull up a map."

Elaina clicked and swiped her fingers on her laptop until a map of the area appeared. She zoomed in until she found the bend in the Rift and the lower parking lot. "The smoke came from somewhere past this area."

"Are there any aerial photos?"

"Not of that side."

"Can you check the archives?"

"I'll try." She typed in map coordinates and soon had an overhead picture of the area. "It's kinda grainy, but it's the right area."

"Okay, I see what we're looking for. See these buildings? I bet he'll spend the night in one of them, so he built a fire. We'll want to intercept him before he gets on the move. Is the drone in your car?"

"Ready to go."

"Then as soon as it's light, we'll look for smoke. You'll grab your laptop and I'll follow you to the lower trailhead by the falls. Do you think there's a place we can get him across? It would save him going through the trees."

Elaina shut down her laptop. "I've scoped out a spot past the falls where the Rift canyon walls are really busted up. I don't know if that's good or bad. We could launch the drone from there and check it out with the cameras."

Roberto gathered up the cables. "I think I should be the one operating the drone for that. You're better at spotting. I'll be preoccupied with running the controls. We'll hook up the laptop so you can control your own view."

"Could we take a high elevation shot first, to see where the smoke is coming from?"

"And see if we can spot Arcon?" said her father, in a teasing voice. "He may be close to there."

"I like the way you think, Dad."

"Then we'd better get some sleep and get an early start."

CHAPTER EIGHTEEN

SATURDAY

Arcon was thankful for his goatskin rug. But the fire had been out for a while, and now he wished he had two rugs.

There were enough embers to start another fire, and soon he was warm again. With nothing to eat, he was eager to get moving. He grabbed his pack, a little wood, and slipped his machete into its scabbard. Before leaving, he tossed a bunch of tire chips on the fire. He thought he could reach the spot he was aiming for by straight up sun.

The grass was so tall he couldn't make out the precise edge of the Rift, but he was getting close. He longed to look into it, to see this thing that restricted the world he knew. He wanted to see . . .

The ground under his feet disappeared. He toppled face-first onto a ledge that was a foot lower than he'd been walking on. Thanks to the grass, his fall had been more frightening than injurious.

He froze, then felt around. With his machete, he sliced at the grass and revealed a foot wide gash in the ground. And he was on the wrong side of it. He jumped back to the mainland, thankful he hadn't fallen into the crack. It appeared to stretch beyond his view in both directions.

He chopped at the grass and followed the crack. It arced, eventually ending at the Rift in both directions. He'd fallen onto a piece of ground completely separated from the mainland. It was larger than the Facility and had dropped a foot from its original location. *Here's a good place to start another signal fire.* He looked toward Calico, but couldn't see the cabins. But he knew if the fire were big enough, Elaina would see it. And with the earth crack to contain it, he could put it out as soon as she contacted him.

"I see it, Dad!" yelled Elaina, "the black smoke!"

"Is it in the same spot as last time?"

"That's affirmative. It's a much larger puff of smoke this time. I'd say it was definitely intentional."

"All right, girl, let's move."

Arcon cut grass away from the crack and threw it as far as he could onto the detached area of land. He snapped off some dead blackberry vines and lit them on fire. When the ends were burning well, he tossed them onto the detached land.

It took a while, but the grass caught fire and started to spread. The grass was moist from the recent rains, burning slow and making a lot of smoke. *Okay, Elaina, I've done my part. Find me!* While he waited, he kept cutting grass away from the earth crack to feed the fire.

Soon half the detached land was on fire, creating a huge plume of smoke. *This will certainly get a response from somebody.*

Roberto and Elaina pretended to struggle with the drone when in view of onlookers. For a Saturday, the parking lot wasn't very busy; mostly hikers who moved on. Before others could arrive, Elaina grabbed the drone and ran with it. Roberto moved his vehicle to the trailhead. He watched Elaina disappear down the trail.

While the drone was visible in the air, he could operate it up to five kilometers away. Down inside the Rift that range would drop to a half kilometer. All of that depended on using the direction transmitter in the SRV. The mobile omni-directional transmitter would be too risky down in a deep canyon. He had plenty of cameras to see what was around it, but that was no good if he couldn't control it.

He grabbed the radio. "Are you about ready down there?"

"Just a second while I get clear," she answered. "By the way, I'm about ten meters from the edge. Okay, fire it up."

He waited, then watched his view screen as the blades revved and the drone rose to a meter off the ground. "Everything checks out. Come on back." He raised the drone, shot toward the Rift, and dropped into it.

Elaina yelled, "Woo-hoo!"

When she got back to the SRV, her dad said, "You gotta see this."

"Let me get set up." Elaina turned on her laptop, handed the tiny cord to her dad, and plugged in her end. The screen flashed to life and auto-loaded the drone camera software. After a minute, she had the same view her dad did, with one camera looking down into the Rift in the center of the screen, and eight small screens around it, giving her a panoramic view from inside the Rift. "Wow, I have so wanted to do this." She tapped on one view after another to fill the screen.

"You and me both," said Roberto.

"What do you think so far?" she asked. "Can he cross here?"

"I don't know. I wouldn't do it, but I'm not desperate. Baby girl, I don't like anything about this."

"So you still prefer the freeway?"

"It'd be a walk in the park compared to this. There, we'd need three hundred meters of rope. This crossing would take at least a thousand. We have the rope, but getting it to Arcon would be difficult."

"Wow! Would you look at how the sides of the Rift bulge in and out? This wasn't a clean break."

"No, it wasn't. Wish I could see the bottom. Wait. I have an idea." Roberto flipped a switch on the controller to turn on the lights. "Yep, the lights are reflecting off the bottom. It's covered with water. He may have to swim."

"Have you seen enough of the Rift?"

"Eager to go overland, are we?"

"Yes, please, before we wear down the capacitors."

"Oh, we could stay down here a lot longer. You know these are super caps. They'll last a good long time. Plus, I bet you have another set all charged up."

Elaina rolled her eyes. "Okay, now you're messing with me. Can we get moving? And turn off those lights!"

Roberto flew the drone south inside the Rift to keep it out of the public's view. When it was safe, he brought it up where he could see it.

Elaina yelled, "Dad, look! Do you see it? No, don't hover. Move it south, south, south. Quite a ways. Do you see it? Look at the smoke down there. That's right on the edge of the Rift. Go down there."

"Backseat flyer," said Roberto.

"It could be a bonfire ... or is it a grass fire?" she said, ignoring him. "Go higher."

"We'll attract attention."

"I think that fire is already going to. We'll need to work fast now."

"Better come back for the contact package."

"Not until I see his face, Dad. Please."

Arcon was chopping grass when he heard what sounded like a swarm of bees overhead. He flattened himself on the ground. The sun was blinding. He saw something in the sky, but couldn't make out what it was. He scrambled to his feet and ran for cover. He slipped in a hole and regained his footing, but the sound was closing in fast on his position. He dodged and fell again.

"There he is!" They watched a man running and stumbling. "You're scaring him, Dad! Back off, back off. Wait till he settles down."

Roberto brought the drone up to a hover at about 100 meters. The man fell again and just lay there, staring up at the drone. They watched him raise his forearm.

"Rock the drone, Dad. Wave at him!"

Roberto wiggled the lever, and the drone rocked side to side. The man just stared. Then he waved.

Elaina felt tears welling. "That's him, Daddy, that's him!" She started to cry. "That's Arcon!"

They drew closer, but Arcon got up as if to run away. Roberto stopped and hovered. "You sure that's him?" asked Roberto. "He looks like a caveman."

"That's him, Daddy. Let's bring the drone back for the contact package. I want to talk to him."

Arcon hoped Elaina was controlling whatever that thing was that was flying overhead. He worried it was some kind of automatic fire control device he'd triggered. *Oh, my fire! Can't let it jump to the mainland.*

He ran back to the broken-off area of land. The wind was pushing the flames close to the mainland. He jumped over the crack and stomped out the flames burning east, and left the Rift side of the fire to burn out on its own.

He jumped back to the mainland. The buzzing was gone. He looked around but didn't see the thing anywhere in the sky.

He slumped to the ground. *It wasn't Elaina. Probably some kind of fire patrol. I wonder if I'll get reported to the authorities? Maybe Elaina got caught and the authorities are looking for me. Maybe I should run for the woods while I have a chance.*

At this point it didn't matter. He would sit it out and deal with whatever the future held. *God, give me strength.*

Elaina ran down the trail, carrying a box with a light-gauge paracord attached to it. Her dad maneuvered the drone near her and shut it off. Once the props stopped, Elaina turned the drone over and installed a fresh set of super-capacitors and tied the paracord to its underbelly. She carefully rolled the drone upright, strung the paracord trailings well away, and yelled, "Clear—fire up!"

Roberto started the drone's props and it slowly gained elevation. At about fifteen meters the paracord grew taut and lifted the box.

Elaina tugged lightly on the paracord and said, "Package secure. Deliver it!"

Roberto noticed that cars were collecting in the parking lot. *Too late now.* He flew the drone straight up and took off to where he'd last seen the man in animal skins. When he didn't spot anyone, he headed for the fire.

Elaina climbed into the SRV and grabbed her laptop. "Have you found him?"

"Not yet—"

"Look! There he is!" A man had emerged from amongst the tall grass.

Roberto hovered the drone from a distance, then eased it down, lowering the package. "I hope he knows what to do with it."

Arcon's heart raced when he heard the buzzing noise again. He knew his life would change in the next few moments. He frantically searched the sky for the source of the sound. This time he would stand his ground. *If I'm in trouble with the authorities, so be it. But if it's Elaina—*

He spotted the object. Hanging down from it was something cubicle, connected by a small rope to the buzzing thing. When he could reach it, he untied it, and the buzzing thing took off.

He looked the box over and saw Morse code that read: [Open ME CAREFULLY].

CHAPTER NINETEEN

Derik greeted Jarden as he climbed the tree into the Sunset Outpost. He'd expected Jarden to be back with a wayward hunter in tow—but here he was with nothing, looking like he'd been dragged through the jungle. "You need a shower."

With a heavy breath, Jarden replied, "Food first."

"I have the distinct feeling you couldn't persuade him to return."

"You know he's a good kid. He just has a very strong will."

"Oh, he has that," said Derik, handing him a strip of goat jerky. "You know, I was tempted to let him go myself."

"Personally, I'm glad you didn't," said Jarden, as he plopped himself in a crudely built chair made of tree limbs. "I've watched that kid his whole life. His folks and I were real close, rest their souls. But they didn't appreciate me taking him under my wing and teaching him to hunt. They wanted him to work in the lab with them. But his heart was never in it."

"I wish my son would've wanted to be a hunter instead of a metalworker."

Jarden sat motionless, staring at nothing in particular. "He's a tad different, that boy."

"Who, my son?" asked Derik.

"No, no ... Arcon," clarified Jarden.

Derik nodded. "Oh, right. I know what you mean."

"But I think he's different in a good way. Arcon pushes himself to understand, and when he feels things aren't right, he pushes back. That kind of person is difficult to be around in a world like ours. Maybe it's time we got ourselves prepared for a new dynamic."

"So you think he'll make it to the outside world?"

Jarden looked out across the expanse of trees. "He says he has someone to help him get across the Rift. That's why he went that way. And he says God is asking him to do it. If that's the case, you know he'll make it."

"We knew it'd happen someday. But I thought the consensus was we all stay or all go at once. A lot of people will be on edge with him out there."

"I told him to use his better judgment about bringing the outside world into this place. His plan is to let us know the truth about what's out there. Although I think he may get distracted."

"You may be right." Derik nodded. "I hope you're right— about getting distracted, I mean. Sentiment is still hard against outsiders."

"But Derik, no one living has ever met an outsider. It's only the rumors they don't trust, not the flesh and blood. If the folks outside are still crazy, I told Arcon to leave us be. If he can't handle it, I said he could bring the girl back, but nobody else. I have faith. He's got God in his heart, Derik. Strong too."

Derik buried his head in his hands. "I know it's my job, but I sure would appreciate it if you'd break this to the Community."

"Be glad to," said Jarden. "But I think I'll rest here for a bit before I swing back to the Facility. Have any more jerky?"

"I have a few more pieces. The boys ate the rest."

"That'll be fine. Are you going to stay out here, or are you headed back?"

"I'll go back with you. Want me to snag the other swing for you?"

"Could you?"

"No problem. I'll be back in a few. You just sit and figure out what to tell the Community. I told the boys not to say a word."

"Thanks Derik. Tell you what, have the procurement team meet me in the Franklin room in a couple hours."

"That's a good idea. The boys won't stay quiet for long."

"We should probably include the department heads,"said Jarden. "I'll stop by the Ashford place and talk to Brina on the way in."

"I hadn't thought about her. She won't be happy about this."

"No, but she deserves to hear it from me first."

"Understood. I'll try to keep everything in control until you get back."

"Thanks."

Arcon took out his knife and sliced through the transparent film that held the box together. He opened the flaps, and the first thing he saw was a piece of paper that said, in big letters, **READ THIS FIRST**. He unfolded the paper:

Hi Arcon,

If you're reading this, you are almost home! Our home that is. I can't wait to welcome you to our world and find out more about yours. And you. But I don't want to write much more. I want you to hear my voice. We can do that right now.

Inside is a small box with something I need you to stick in your ear. Then push the red button and you'll finally be able to hear my voice. Built into this device is a microphone, so when you speak, I'll be able to hear yours too. Sorry, but Morse code was getting old.

Find the small box and open it carefully. Please do not drop the device you find inside or get it wet. There is some food and a vitamin drink inside. If you need it, eat it. But not too much at a time. It's highly concentrated survival food.

He was eager to read the rest and eat something, but he was dying to hear Elaina's voice. He rummaged through the package, found the small box, and set it on his open pack.

He took a quick look at the other items in the box, focusing on a clear container filled with a pale red liquid. The top wouldn't pull off. He looked closely and saw threads like a bolt. He twisted it, heard it crackle, and twisted more until it was off. It smelled fruity. He put a little on his finger, tasted it, and then with full abandon took three full swallows.

Curiosity satisfied, he went back to the small box, opened it, and dug through some strange material until he found a small silvery object. He looked it over, wondering how the entire thing would fit in his ear. He went back to Elaina's note.

When you've opened the little box, look at the device. On one end, you'll see a funny-shaped piece that is clear and soft. This part goes in your ear. On the other side is a small red button that turns the device on. Stick the soft part of the device in your ear and press the red button. When you do, it will signal me. I'll say something to you, and when you hear it, all you have to do is talk to me. Now please do it. I'm eager to hear your voice.

Arcon positioned the device near his ear and pushed. He twisted it in a few different angles and pushed harder, afraid it would fall out. He finally gave it one more push, not realizing he'd pressed the red button.

He was in the process of intentionally pressing the button when he heard "Can you hear…" and then silence. He looked around, then waited for more. He looked back at his instructions and tried pressing the button again. "Can you hear me, Arcon?"

He planned to respond, but when he heard her voice he just dropped to his knees and said, "Thank you, Lord."

He could hear emotion in her voice as she responded, "Amen to that." Then there was a moment of silence. Finally, she went on. "Arcon," she said. "Welcome to our world. This is Elaina."

It overwhelmed Arcon. Her voice was crisp and clear. Not raspy and broken, as with the crystal radio he'd tried so long ago. She had a pleasant, welcoming voice. But it still seemed strange without seeing her face. He thought about that for a moment, then joked, "Pleased to meet your voice, Elaina. But I would like to get to the other side of this hole in the ground so I can see your face. Got any ideas?"

Elaina held the microphone toward her dad, who said, "Hey, Arcon, buddy, this is Roberto, Elaina's father. How are you doing over there?"

It surprised Arcon to hear a different voice in his head. "Mr. Roberto sir, glad to meet you. Thank you for helping Elaina with this. I'm hungry and quite perforated, but I'm suddenly feeling a lot better."

Elaina hit the mute button. "What does he mean by 'perforated'?" Roberto shrugged. Elaina asked, "Arcon, what does 'perforated' mean?"

"It means I'm full of holes from the needle brush. But don't worry. None of it is life threatening."

"Understood, Arcon," said Roberto. "I tell you buddy, we have two plans to get you out of there. One is bad, and the other is, well, a bit worse, from our perspective, anyway. We want to tell you about them both and let you decide."

"Tell you what. I'll let you folks talk in my head while I sample some of this food. Is this like an MRE?"

"What is an MRE?" asked Elaina.

"I don't know," said Arcon. "Some kind of survival food. We had a remembrance room at our facility where we kept things from the founder days. There was this package that said *MRE, Meals Ready to Eat, Vegetarian*, and then it had military stuff on it."

Roberto spoke up. "That's probably why we haven't heard about it. We haven't had a military since …"

Elaina hit the mute button. "Dad, we promised not to give Arcon too much information about this place until we get him in it."

"Oh, yeah, sorry." He pointed at the mute button and Elaina pressed it. "Yes, it's a lot like MRE. It has a lot of nutrition and calories, so you don't have to carry as much."

"Arcon," Elaina interjected, "Try the one that says double-chocolate chip. You'll like that one."

"Uh, okay, here, I found it. Uh, it looks like, well, something you wouldn't want to step in."

"Just trust me. I haven't failed you yet, have I?"

"Sorry, you'll have to speak up. I'm chewing. I hope you have more of this chip stuff out there. Our chips were, uh, fuel."

Elaina hit the mute button while her dad roared with laughter. He said, "Do you think he meant wood chips or cow chips? We gotta get this guy over here." Elaina's hair danced as she nodded enthusiastically. She looked past him to the parking lot. Her dad turned to see what had caught her eye. A handful of people were pointing at them from the parking lot, and others at the still-rising smoke in the distance.

"Whatever we do, we'd better do it quick."

Elaina unmuted and said, "Arcon, we have a situation over here. It seems we're attracting more attention than we want."

"Are you in trouble?"

Roberto whispered, "I have an idea," then said, "Arcon, listen to me. I think the people in Calico can see the smoke."

"I'm familiar with Calico. You spent the night there, right?"

Roberto saw Elaina shrug her shoulders. "That's right. Anyway, what we'll do is pack up the drone and go up to Elaina's cabin. We'll talk to you as we go. If we stay away for an hour, the crowd should disperse. Meanwhile, put out that fire and stop the smoke. If you hear a noise, hide. It may not be our drone."

"Right, got it. What's a drone?"

"The thing that brought you the package," said Elaina. "We gotta go. Love ya."

Arcon jumped up to go put out the fire, which was mostly now just the last of the grass on the detached area. He stopped. *She loves me?*

Ranger Dan scanned the forest past the waterfall, trying to spot a fire someone had reported. Ranger Becca said they'd received several calls, so he assumed there should be something there. Otherwise he wouldn't have climbed all the way up to the observation tower.

The rain that went through didn't have any lightning associated with it. There could be hikers down that direction, but no campfires were allowed. If a fire had started, then it must have put itself out. He sat and rested where he could watch, just in case. *Father, if there's something down there I need to be aware of, open my eyes to see it.*

He tapped his shoulder phone and said, "Call Becca."

"CalNeva Ranger Station, Ranger Becca speaking."

"Did you get any more calls on the fire?"

"Oh, hi Dan. No, I haven't."

"Did anyone give you any information besides seeing smoke?"

"One person said they saw some Search and Rescue people down that direction flying around a drone. The drone took off toward the smoke. They said the drone came back, and the searchers left with it. That was twenty minutes ago."

"We never got a message from San Bernardino?"

"Nothing."

"Let me know when we do. They're probably busy on the weekend."

"Probably so. I'll call you if I hear from them or get any more reports of smoke."

"That'll be good. I've seen nothing yet. I'll wait here a little longer, then come back to the station."

"See you then. Bye."

CHAPTER TWENTY

When Elaina and her dad were set up in their cabin, they tried contacting Arcon again. "Arcon, can you hear me?"asked Elaina.

"Okay, I can hear you now. I think I lost you for a while."

"We were driving in the hills, but we're in the cabin now and have a line of sight in your direction. We should be fine here."

"Great. I got the fire out."

"Hey, buddy," said Roberto. "Sorry we can't airlift you out of there with a man-chopper."

"A man-chopper?" asked Arcon. "I don't like the sound of that!"

Roberto laughed. "It's like a drone that's large enough to carry a person. They're big and loud. We gotta get you out of there more discreetly."

"Okay. So, what's Plan B?"

"Actually, that was … never mind," stammered Roberto. "The Rift where you're at is very wide and probably very deep. You'd have to use a rope to climb down, swim to the other side, and then we'd set up ropes on our side so you could climb back out. Make sense?"

"Uhhh … hmm. I climb trees all the time. But I don't know how to swim. What's Plan C?"

"Crossing at the freeway."

"That was actually Plan A," piped in Elaina. "If you would've come down the I-15 like you were supposed to!"

"Sorry," said Arcon. "I had a bit of a sticky situation on this side."

"No problem," said Elaina. "Just giving you a bad time."

Arcon laughed. "Not too bad so far. So what's this about crossing at the freeway?"

"Our digital measure reads 160 meters across the broken ends of the freeway. You'd still need to climb down and back up, but we could use a continuous set of ropes. You could hang onto it while you're in the water. But you'd have to get through the forest to get there. Arcon, there are wolves in the forest, and the sticker brush looks impenetrable."

"I've never run into wolves, but they're probably like coyotes. You just need to let them have their own space. Hmmm, let me think about it. How much is 160 meters in feet?"

"Uhh ... about 500 feet."

"How much rope do you have?"

"As much as you need. What are you thinking?" asked Roberto.

"I'm liking plan C," said Arcon. "If I can get to the trees, I'm not worried about the wolves or the needle-brush."

"I don't know what you're thinking," said Roberto. "Those stickers could rip you to shreds."

"Trust me," said Arcon. "They won't be a problem. But I need to climb into the trees to avoid them. While I'm doing that, can you make me a super-rope?"

"A what?"

Over a hundred people were packed into the Franklin meeting room; a fraction of the ArcPoint Community. Most were part of the Procurement Team, responsible for organizing the physical needs of the Community. The others were leaders within ArcPoint, chosen to pass messages down to their various groups.

Jarden stood in front and tried to appear calm. "If you can all find a seat, we'll get started," he said, in a coarse but booming voice. "Derik, could you start us with a word to our Lord?"

Derik moved to the front and when the noise settled down, said, *"Father, we thank you for the tight-knit community you've created here. You've kept us safe, as you promised. You've supplied our needs and kept us united as one. Supply to us today that singular communication by your one and only spirit, speaking at this time through your servant Jarden. Amen."*

As Derik spoke, Jarden scanned the room. He was glad to see Brina wasn't amongst them. He wanted to tell her the news about Arcon privately. No one had been home when he'd stopped at the Ashford log cabin. The hemp workers said she'd gone out for a walk with her grandfather.

"As I look around the room," Jarden began, "I see many of my fellow hunters. Some of you are too old to swing, others are too young to do it correctly." The people laughed and pointed at each other.

"As many of you have already guessed, we are here to discuss, and I believe to honor, Arcon Franklin, whose ancestor this room is named after. He is the descendant of a Founder, he was one of my best hunters, and he was my friend." Jarden could tell by the crowd's murmur that many hadn't heard the news, and very few knew as much as he did.

"I was the last person to talk to Arcon. I want to share with you his plan, and his rationale, as I heard it straight from his own voice. To begin with, he will no longer be a part of the Community, physically. But in spirit he'll remain united with us. God is in him as He is in you. Keep that in mind before all things.

"Second, he has connected with an outsider—a woman he believes serves God the Creator as we do. He has communicated with her for nearly eight years and is now on his way to find her. He believed it possible to find a wife here, but that God wanted him to look outside this forest. He holds hope, but not certainty, for a union to take place with this outsider. He asks for your prayers for God's guidance in this endeavor, as he asked for mine.

"Lastly, he has another reason for leaving the security of this forest to enter the uncertainty of the outside world. He feels called by God to investigate whatever is out there. He realizes the Community is not officially sending him, so he will not be claiming to represent us. In the future, he hopes to return to this place and report on his findings. At that time, he'll determine what the future holds for him and allow the Community to do the same. He's agreed to not bring the outside world into our forest. The guidance of this community by the Holy Spirit is still his first loyalty. With this act he gives his life for it. Our prayers should be that his life is a long one."

The reaction from the people was somber. Jarden had expected as much, but hoped a few would be excited for Arcon to find a life partner. This response felt to him more like a funeral than a wedding. Then again, Arcon had broken with tradition and rejected the Community. How could people rejoice about that? He hoped a few would pray for Arcon, and that no one would curse him.

Raymo scowled and left the Franklin meeting room. Now he knew it was Arcon he'd seen running into the forest.

Raymo often studied stories of evil in the outside world. He cherished the peace and fellowship they enjoyed at ArcPoint and dedicated himself to keeping it that way. That's why he volunteered as a night guard.

For a long time, he'd considered Arcon reckless. Rebellious. Even foolish. What young man in his right mind would reject Brina Ashford as a life partner? Now that same senseless person might succeed at joining the outside world. They'll find out from him that ArcPoint is defenseless.

He was glad Chad told him about the meeting. He understood it was meant for the hunters who'd worked with Arcon and to inform the leaders. *But Keenan should have invited me anyway. I was the one who discovered him leaving.*

Arcon was getting frustrated with his attempts to reach the ArcPoint trees. Whenever he got close, a wolf would come out to challenge him. *It's the nasty time, he thought. It has pups to protect.* At least he knew it wasn't considering him for a meal. He tried moving further from the Rift, but only encountered a different wolf.

He had insisted on shutting off the earpiece and putting it in his pouch. Elaina got upset with him for even suggesting it, and he'd said he was sorry, but had done it anyway. He'd reconnect when he was safely in the trees. If anything happened to him, he didn't want her experiencing the sound of it. But now he needed her help. He turned his earpiece back on. *Why isn't she responding?*

Elaina and Roberto tied ropes together to make something long enough to reach across the Rift. After lengthening, they braided the sections together, as Arcon had instructed. He'd explained three ropes braided together would be stronger and easier for him to handle. When it was finished, they wrapped it with one of the paracords for extra security.

Elaina continued to voice her concern about the whole idea. Roberto, on the other hand, knew if this plan didn't work, Arcon would get the blame, not him.

"Do you hear something?" asked Roberto.

"Oh, it's the two-way," said Elaina, moving to the base station. "Arcon's trying to reach us." She pressed a button on the base. "Arcon, do you read me?"

"Well, I hear you, finally. Where were you?"

"Sorry, we were busy making your super-rope thing."

"You've got lots of time. I haven't made it to the trees yet. A wolf won't let me get close. She must be protecting pups."

"Are you okay?"

"Oh, sure. To her I'm just an intruder. I could use your help to scare her off."

"How can we help?"

"Could you fly that drone thing down here and keep her away long enough for me to climb into one of the trees?"

Elaina looked at her dad, who nodded. "We'll be right there. Keep this channel open. Uh, don't turn off your earpiece, okay?"

"Sure, I'll be watching for you."

As the drone reached Arcon's location, they saw a wolf slowly slip out of the trees. "Watch out," yelled Elaina. "There's one coming toward you!"

"I know that," said Arcon. "I'm coaxing her out so you know where she is. I'll stay outside its comfort zone till we're ready. Do you see her at the edge of the trees, Roberto?"

"Be careful, Arcon!" said Elaina.

"I know what I'm doing," snapped Arcon. "Roberto, if you can, come in from behind. Drop down and buzz the drone around the right side of my head. As soon as you do, I'll run right behind it. Fly straight in front of me, directly at her. Try to chase her to the right, not straight into the forest. I'll head for the trees while you keep her occupied. If you're ready, attack!"

"Going now!" said Roberto, and dove the drone toward Arcon. They heard the whine of the drone in the radio as it roared past Arcon's head. They watched the wolf tuck tail and run into the needle-brush.

Roberto maneuvered the drone while Elaina scanned the monitor for any threats. Arcon slashed at the needle brush with his machete like a madman, pushing vines aside with his arms and stomping them with his feet. Roberto lowered the drone and rocked it whenever the wolf moved closer to him. It took quite a few minutes for Arcon to slash through the needle brush, but Roberto deftly kept the drone at his side, even going partway into the forest with him.

Suddenly, Arcon leapt in the air and grabbed a branch. Roberto and Elaina couldn't believe what they were seeing on the screen. With a quick pull and a flip, Arcon was standing on a branch, waving at them. "I'm okay, I'm okay. Leave!"

They stared in amazement for a moment, and then Roberto carefully flew the drone out of the trees and back to their spot at the parking lot.

As Roberto packed the drone, Elaina asked Arcon, "Are you okay?"

"I'm fine," he said. "I'm bleeding, so I'll sit and do some skin patching. Don't worry, I've seen worse."

"Leave the earpiece on."

"Okay. How far of a run is it to the freeway?"

"Five kilometers, or about three miles. But save your energy. No need to run."

"Oh, sorry. Running is what we call moving down the branches. Never mind, I'll explain it later. Tell you what. I have a bright yellow vest I wear hunting. I'll put it on and stay in the trees near the Rift. Maybe you can see what I mean. I'll turn off the earpiece and stop every so often and check in. Will that work?"

"That'll work for us, Arcon." She heard her dad shut the back of the SRV. "Dad is ready to move out. We're heading back to the cabin to finish your super-rope. Be safe. Love ya!"

Arcon turned off his earpiece. The wolf was pacing below him. He pondered what Elaina just said. *Love you. Maybe it means something different in the outside world.*

CHAPTER TWENTY-ONE

"Dan, Ranger Dwight is on the phone for you."

"Okay, thanks Becca."

Ranger Dan pressed line two. "Hi Dwight, watcha need?"

"Becca told me to stop by the lower trailhead and check things out. Told me about a fire alert. Anyway, I saw the Search and Rescue folks and they were flying the drone again. I asked what they were doing. They said they were testing it. When I asked if they'd checked out the fire, and they acted like they didn't know what I was talking about. They just now drove off with the drone. Thought you'd wanna know."

"That's strange. Someone said the drone flew toward the smoke."

"That's what I heard too, from Becca."

"Okay, well, keep your eyes open. Let me know if you see them again."

"Will do, sir."

As soon as Jarden could get away from the meeting, he headed straight for the hydroponics shack. Both of Brina's parents worked there, and it was her Grandpa Lars favorite place to go. It really was beautiful this time of year, with all the flowers and new spring growth. He hated to spoil their time together.

Lars Ashford was nearly a hundred and twenty years old and the only person left who'd known all the Founders. His father was Dr. Norman Ashford, the one who designed the hydroponic garden, the greenhouse, and practically every other aspect of plant production for the ArcPoint community. Lars may be Brina's grandfather, but he was more like her best friend. Usually, if you found one Ashford, the other was nearby.

Jarden found Lars in the tomato area with her parents, Thomas and Sybil. "Is Brina around here somewhere?"

"She's out in the hemp area, tending to her babies," said Sybil.

"Okay, thanks."

Jarden walked outside and headed for the large green plants. This industrial hemp made his job easy, since so many products could be made from it. From soap to ropes, sheets to shoes, and curtains to building insulation, he depended a lot on the skills of the hemp workers. He hated to consider what their lives would be like, had the Founders rejected these plants.

In the early days, the Community had been so frightened of being invaded they wanted nothing to attract others to their location. Even though it had no hallucinogenic qualities, plants that looked like marijuana could bring in undesirable people. But they couldn't get cotton to grow well, and the goats couldn't provide enough wool or leather.

Lee Franklin convinced them it wasn't fair to condemn something God created because mankind had corrupted it. If the Community needed the hemp, they would ask God to protect them so they could use it.

Brina's main job was to harvest the seeds and grow the seedlings. Others helped her during planting season, and then she made sure the hemp stayed healthy. Since that wasn't hard to do, she spent a lot of time helping the hemp workers, assisting in the dye house, or caring for her grandpa.

Jarden looked around the hemp area, but with the plants already twelve feet tall he couldn't see Brina. He walked around, looking down each row. He called, "Brina, are you out here somewhere?"

"Over here, Jarden."

He walked a little farther and spotted her in the middle of a row. "There you are. I need to talk with you."

"Sure, just a minute."

He saw her tamping the soil down around one of the plants, so he asked, "Did Toddler get loose again?"

"Sure did. I'd let that silly goat eat the plants if he wanted, but he likes to jerk them out of the ground."

Jarden chuckled. "Maybe we'll have to make some more jerky one of these days."

Brina turned and shook her finger at him. "Don't be doing that. He's one of my favorites, except for the fact he likes the young hemp plants." As she walked toward him she asked, "What did you need to talk about?"

He waited till she got closer, then said, "Arcon."

"What about him?"

Jarden glanced at the ground, then back at her. "Can we find a place to sit down?"

"Sure, we can go back to Hydro."

"I'd rather we discussed this alone for right now."

"If you don't mind sitting on a log, we can go to the other end of the row."

"That'd be fine. Lead the way."

Brina walked down the row of tall hemp plants. "You're making me nervous. Is Arcon okay?"

"Oh, he's fine. I'm sure of it."

They rounded the end of the row and walked to a rough-hewn table flanked by two logs. "Have a seat. This is where I start the seedlings. Is this okay?"

"Perfectly fine." Jarden sat opposite her at the table and folded his arms. "Arcon left the Community a few days ago."

Her eyes got big. "What do you mean by that?"

"You know how he talked about going to the outside world? Well, he finally did it."

"How do you know?"

"The hunters tracked him for two days. I finally caught up to him this morning and we had a talk."

"I … I just talked to him. He said nothing to me about leaving."

"I know. He lied to me about it as well. But you know if he'd told us we would've stopped him. So I understand he couldn't risk it. Still hurts though, doesn't it?"

Brina turned away. Stared at the hemp plants. "He's been sort of distant for a while. Now I know why." They sat in silence. Brina rubbed away a tear. "That's why he was ordering the hemp ropes too, wasn't it?"

"Yeah. Hate to say it, but that was his plan all along, to use them to get out of here."

Turning back, she asked, "Which way did he go?"

"Toward the Rift."

"You're kidding. What's he thinking?"

"Someone on the outside is supposed to help him get across." He looked into her eyes. "Did you know anything about a radio he was using?"

"When we were kids, yeah. He put together something he called a crystal radio from plans in a book. He let me listen to it a few times, but I didn't hear much."

"He figured out some way to talk to people out there. Connected with someone who eventually agreed to help him."

"You didn't know about any of this until yesterday?" asked Brina.

Jarden hung his head. "He told me about wanting to leave. I thought I'd talked him out of it, so I didn't say anything. I gave him some time to think it over. Thought that's what he was doing."

"Yeah, that makes sense. I found him wandering around the tiny houses and he wouldn't tell me why." She turned toward the plantings. "He didn't even say goodbye."

"Brina, listen. I know for a fact you were his first choice here for a life partner. He told me so. But he also said he knew you wouldn't want to go with him, and he felt God was calling him to leave. We have to trust Arcon and trust God to take care of him. Can you be at peace with that?"

She turned back toward Jarden. "To be honest, I know you're right. Years ago we discussed leaving together, and I told him I had no desire to do that. I still don't. I love this place. I'd never leave Grandpa. I'll miss Arcon, but I want him to be where he's supposed to be."

"I hope you mean that."

"Why?"

"He seriously thinks this outsider may be a life partner for him."

"You're kidding! It's a girl?"

"Yeah. Sorry about that. He told me he's been communicating with a girl for a few years."

"How *many* years?"

"He said it was eight years ago when they first connected. I know, strange, isn't it? That he could keep it hidden from us for this long? To be honest, I think God has been helping him. After talking to him I have a peace that he's doing something God put in his heart to do." Then he looked in her eyes and said, "He'll be okay. We need to let him go."

Brina turned away from him again. Her lips quivered as she fought back the tears. She looked back at him. "I can do that." She smiled. "Let's look on the bright side. People will stop trying to get me to marry him. Grandpa never liked Arcon for me, anyway. You haven't told him yet, have you?"

"Who, your grandpa? No, I haven't told your family anything yet. But I did tell the hunters and the procurement team. They needed to know. I plan to get the whole Community together. I should probably get going so I can work on my speech. A lot of folks may not be too happy."

"My grandpa will be one of them. But don't worry. I'll tell him."

"Great, thanks." Jarden stood. "It's been good talking with you, Brina. Hope you don't mind if we speak more often, now that Arcon's gone."

"I'd like that. I'll pray that God gives you good words for the meeting."

"Thanks."

CHAPTER TWENTY-TWO

Elaina and her dad finished wrapping the ropes with paracord. They'd staggered the ends so the knots wouldn't be at the same location on the assembly. Once in a while they'd see if they could spot Arcon in the monitor, but had only seen him once, so far. "Would you like to stop for dinner?" asked Elaina, more for a chance to search for Arcon than for a meal.

"Sure, we can inspect this later."

"How soon do you think it'll be before he knocks off for the day? I hope he doesn't push it too hard."

"He knows what he's doing," said Roberto, as he walked over to look at the big screen on the table. "Elaina, look at this," he said, grabbing the remote. "He's clear over here." He moved the telescope and focused in. "Look at him move!"

"Unbelievable," said Elaina. "He's literally running down those branches. Look. He gets to the trunk, moves around to another branch, and off he goes. Oh, my! He just jumped to a different tree. I can't watch. I'm going to make us dinner."

"I've gotta watch," said Roberto.

Elaina shook her head. "Somehow I'm not surprised."

"Well, I think I'm figuring it out. He climbs higher so he can jump to a lower branch on the next tree. Brilliant. Looks like he's stopped to plot a course. No, he's reaching for his pack. I think you're about to get a call from a secret admirer."

Elaina dropped the microwaveable dinner and hurried over to the base station. No signal. She looked at the big screen. In the shadows she saw Arcon's yellow vest, but couldn't make out what he was doing. Then the signal came in. She pressed the button on the microphone. "Elaina to Arcon, we see you in the trees." She saw him walk out onto a branch.

"Sorry Elaina, I can't see you. The sun is in my eyes."

"That's okay, stay away from the Rift." She muted and said, "Boy, he makes me nervous."

Arcon answered back, "Should I climb the tree so you can see me better?"

"No, no, you're fine."

"Am I half way yet?"

"You're about three-quarters of the way."

"That's good. I need to stop and make a nest."

She muted again and asked her dad, "He needs to do what? Make a nest?" He motioned for her to ask Arcon. "Did you say you have to make a nest?"

"Yes, you know—a nest. With branches, a home, a bed. Like a bird. You have birds, don't you?"

"Yes, we have birds. But humans don't build nests."

"I guess they don't live in trees. I'll sleep in a tree tonight. I have to build a bed, otherwise I'll fall and surprise a wolf."

"Okay, I see. Makes sense."

"I'll talk to you again before I sleep. I'm going now."

"Just a minute," interrupted Roberto. "We've got the telescope trained on your position. After you build the nest, take off your vest so others don't spot you."

"Okay," he said, "I'll make the nest first, so you know where I am. I am going now. Love you."

Roberto looked at his daughter. "Sounds like you're getting to him."

"I haven't been leading him on. Honest."

"Elaina, it's okay. Just take it easy. Be careful and go slow.

He seems like a good young man, even if he *is* dressed like a wild one."

They watched as Arcon chopped at branches and laid them out across two others. He was even clearing an opening in their direction, whether to see or be seen they didn't know.

Elaina microwaved their dinner. When she returned, Arcon was in the top of the tree, reaching way out. "I sure wish he wouldn't do that, Dad"

"I think he's getting some food," he responded. "He probably ate what you gave him."

"We should have taken him another package of supplies."

"He'll be fine. We'll take him to a restaurant tomorrow and really show him a thing or two."

"Mexican!" suggested Elaina.

"I was thinking sushi," said Roberto, and they both laughed.

They were just finishing dinner when Arcon signaled. "Are you settled into your nest?" asked Elaina.

"Tweet, tweet," came the response. "Just us bunny birds waiting for first light."

Elaina asked her dad, "What in the world are bunny birds?"

They heard Arcon reply, "I think you call them hawks."

Elaina mouthed, "Oops," to her dad, then said, "They must eat rabbits."

"No, they eat rodents," said Arcon. "We call them bunny birds because they help us find the rabbits. I found a funny stick in the box. What's that?"

Elaina gave her dad a blank look, then remembered. "We call that pepperoni. You eat it."

"I could read that. I didn't know what pepperoni was. I'll try it."

"There's something else in the box you need to know about—" said Roberto.

"The pepperoni is flavorful, and juicier than goat jerky. Not as good as chocolate chips, but I like it," said Arcon.

"Don't eat it all at once," cautioned Elaina.

Robertoleanedintothemicrophone. "Arcon, listen, in the box is a package with something that looks silvery. It says survival blanket."

"I have that in my pack." They heard some rustling. "Here it is. Hmmm. It's not soft like fur. It's not tough like skins."

"Just wrap it around yourself tonight to keep warm."

"Yes, sir. Thanks. The nights have been cold."

"Are you going to sleep now?" asked Elaina.

"Yes. I'll start again at first light, after I eat the rest of the pepperoni. Can you see me okay without the vest?"

They looked at the monitor, but couldn't tell where he was. "Wave your hand."

"I'm right here," he said.

"Okay," said Elaina. "We see you. But it's almost impossible if you're not moving. That's perfect. Sleep tight, and we'll be watching for your signal in the morning."

There was silence for a while. Then Arcon said, "Okay, I'll sleep tight. I'll signal you in the morning. I'm going now."

Roberto looked at his daughter and said, "He sounds confused."

Arcon knew he needed to sleep, but it was still too light out. He was used to a dense, dark forest, but this nest had no trees at all to the west. There was still enough light to read by, so he grabbed the journal.

He opened the book from the back this time, hoping to discover his Grandpa Lee's final thoughts, but was drawn to a section titled:

Remembering.

Something happened today during my daily tour around ArcPoint. Usually I'm struck by all the things we have.

This was a barren desert when we moved here, but God has blessed us with abundance and the skills to meet our needs.

Today was different; I realized all the things we don't have. No cell phones or email or Internet. That means no distractions or scams or robocalls. There are no cars or trucks or motorcycles, which means no traffic and noise. There are no drugs, alcohol, pornography, or any other addiction. There is no theft or murder or violent conflict. There are no taxes because there is no government.

God convicted me big time with that last one. As a government contractor, I learned how to make a profit by bending the rules. I knew where I could cut corners, and which inspectors I had to bribe to do it. Only God knows how many people died in the earthquakes because of the way I built the buildings.

I've told no one the true reason I wanted to flee the city. For others it was the lawlessness, the corruption, or maybe the traffic. For me it was the memories. I didn't want to remember the way I was before I met Jesus. My selfishness put money in my pocket at the expense of other's lives. And because I built schools, those lives could be young.

Today I remembered it all. I saw the buildings, the weak foundations, and the people who walked those halls without fear. They put their faith in me, and I deserved none of it.

Thankfully, the Holy Spirit not only convicts but also teaches and comforts. I remembered how the guilt caused me to put a gun to my head. And I remembered Victoria telling me God could forgive whatever made me do it. He did.

God gave me this responsibility, this new place to build things right. Here there was no one to inspect my work, yet I labored to do everything correctly. I did it out of love for the people who would live in these homes. And I did it for the one who gave me that love and spared my life. I didn't do it for money, which is one more thing ArcPoint doesn't have. No income, banks, or bills.

That reminds me. Competition. In the outside world it was always us against them in sports, business, politics, and religion. That selfish nature polarized everyone. I'm glad it's not here.

When we left, there was a big battle between socialism and capitalism. Neither worked well because some human was always in control of the funds, and they kept too much for themselves. It's much easier to control nothing.

Isn't that a paradox? We have abundance, because we have nothing.

Arcon closed the journal and held it in his arms as he leaned back against the tree. He was now far away from the world he was familiar with, and so close to a place he knew nothing about. He hoped the world outside was different than it used to be. Grandpa Lee hadn't painted a very pretty picture of it.

CHAPTER TWENTY-THREE

SUNDAY

The next morning Arcon awoke and looked toward Calico. He could see the cabins on the hill, but the sun wasn't reflecting from the windows. He climbed to the top of the tree, but the sun wasn't yet high enough.

He climbed back down, put the earpiece in his ear, and hit the power button. He waited. And waited. He folded the survival blanket and put it in his pack. He grabbed the pepperoni. And still he waited.

"Hello Arcon, you got me. This is the worm."

Arcon thought about that. "I don't understand."

"You were obviously the early bird," said Elaina. "Never mind. Did you sleep okay?"

"Tweet, tweet," he replied. Elaina laughed and Arcon enjoyed hearing it.

"How soon are you going to start?"

"Right now. No reason to stay here. Are you through with the super-rope?"

"We're done building it like you told us. When will you tell us what we're doing with it?"

"When I get to the I-15 and the last trees. I'm going now." He was silent a moment, then said, "Love you."

"I love you too, Arcon."

Arcon wasn't sure what to think. Maybe that's how they said goodbye. That phrase wasn't used in ArcPoint unless they meant it. Perhaps she did.

It was still early morning when Arcon reached the last of the trees. An expanse of smooth, gray, patchy ground like the concrete floor of the facility stretched away. And there were other patches. This had to be the I-15.

There was a short wall many feet from the Rift along the barren ground. There were very few berry vines and just a few rhizomes. Best thing was, he hadn't seen the wolf since last night. *This'll be easy.*

He eased down on a branch and put the earpiece in. He pressed the power button. "We see you," came Elaina's voice in his ear. "You're at the freeway."

"I'll get out of the trees and run for those walls," said Arcon.

"Wait till we get there. We're leaving right now."

"I'm okay. The wolf's gone," he said.

"NO, WAIT! Let us get there with the drone, just in case," Elaina pleaded.

"I'm leaving now," he said. "Love you."

Arcon turned off the earpiece, removed it, and tucked it in his pack for safekeeping. Then he walked out onto three different branches before choosing which one to jump from.

Normally he would hang and drop to the ground, but not with wolves in the area. He didn't know what to expect with them. He'd read plenty of stories in the Room of Remembrance, but no one at ArcPoint had ever encountered one. At this point, it wasn't worth taking a risk. He tossed his machete and pack as far as he could toward his intended landing spot, took one last look around the forest, and then jumped as far as he could.

He missed a rhizome by inches, tucked into a ball, and rolled on the ground, stopping just short of another rhizome. He put on his pack and tightened the straps. As he reached for his machete, he heard a snarl from the forest. A wolf, thirty feet away.

Arcon unsheathed the machete and faced the wolf. This one was a male. He still had rhizomes to hack through, the largest he'd ever dealt with. The river nourished the trees well, it seemed.

Every time he turned to hack, the wolf got closer. It seemed more curious than dangerous. He started a routine, hacking and yelling like a madman, then spinning around to face him. He eventually made a hole through the rhizomes and ran to the farthest section of the wall.

On top, he gasped for air and checked his wounds. In the flurry of activity he'd reopened a few of the bad ones and gained a few small cuts. There was nothing for it. He was out of skin patches.

Two people were staring at him from across the Rift. One held a pair of binoculars. The other had her hands on her hips. She pointed to her head.

Elaina and Roberto. They seemed so close. He wished he could jump to their side. Elaina tapped her head again. *Oh, the earpiece.* He reached in his pack and put it in his ear and turned it on.

"No wolves, huh?" asked a voice in his ear.

"Just one," he responded. "He's fine."

"I'm not, you lunkhead. Now, what do we do with this super-rope of yours?"

"Bring me one end of it."

Elaina put her head set on mute. "Now what, Dad? It's too heavy for the drone!"

"Calm down. We'll connect one end of the spare paracord to the super-rope and fly the other end to him. It'll be difficult for him, but actually easier for the drone."

"I thought we used all the paracord on the super-rope."

"I keep an unofficial spare under the seat."

"Now you tell me."

They stretched out the super-rope and attached one end to the paracord. Roberto backed the SRV up to the barricade at the Rift and tied the other end of the super-rope around his bumper.

A crowd was forming. Roberto risked disciplinary action, but donned his Search and Rescue uniform shirt and badge and asked the crowd to move about a hundred meters back from the barricade. He put one big guy in charge of keeping them at a distance.

"Okay girl, I think we're ready. Talk to him."

"Arcon, we're ready to bring you one end of the small rope!"

"Is the other end secure?" asked Arcon.

Elaina looked at her dad and he nodded. "Good to go here!"

"Bring it to me." Arcon heard a faint whirring and saw the drone moving toward him. It slowed when the slack was gone, revved, and sped up again.

"Don't get too close to it," warned Elaina. "We'll set it down. Then you can untie it. Don't let go of the rope or it'll fall into the Rift."

Roberto flew the drone past the barricade, circling the paracord twice around one of the reflector poles. He set the drone down and stopped it. Arcon ran to it and untied the cord. He waved to them and said, "Got it." Roberto started the drone and flew it back across the Rift.

They watched Arcon tie his end to a reflector pole. "Are you ready for me to pull it across?"

"Ready!" said Roberto. "It's up to you now, Arcon. Be careful. It'll get heavy."

Arcon grabbed the cord, went around a second reflector pole, looped it around the pole, and then repeated the process. Each time he finished another loop, more of the super-rope sagged into the Rift.

Arcon was in the midst of making another loop when the bulk of the rope plunged into the Rift. It caught and halted abruptly, sending a ripple across the super-rope to Arcon's side. Arcon stumbled forward, was jerked backward and fell to the ground. The rope dragged him toward the Rift and stopped when the slack was gone.

"Are you okay?" asked Elaina.

"My arm took the brunt of it," said Arcon. "I had it wrapped around the small rope." He looked at his arm and shook it. "Nothing's broken. Let me rest a minute. I think I'll be okay to pull again. Thankfully, it wasn't my strong arm."

Elaina and her dad talked while Arcon sat on the ground for a few minutes. Roberto said, "Well, all the knots held."

"And he didn't end up in the Rift," added Elaina, frowning. "I hope he's okay."

"I'm fine," said Arcon. Elaina realized she'd forgotten to mute again. "The pain is getting less, so I'll start pulling now."

"Don't rush it," responded Elaina.

"It's only pain. Everything still works."

Elaina looked at her dad and shook her head. Roberto spoke quietly. "He's a tough kid. All we can do now is watch."

As Ranger Dan crested the hill, he glanced toward the Rift. *Why are all those people huddled together?* He pulled his ranger vehicle off the road and grabbed his binoculars. Tourists were usually few and scattered at the Freeway Viewpoint. As he focused in, he saw over a dozen facing the Rift. *At least they aren't near it.* A hill blocked his view, so he moved forward to the next pull off.

He could see a vehicle backed up to the barrier wall with writing on the side. He recognized it as a San Bernardino Search and Rescue vehicle. *What in the world?* He adjusted the focus to be sure he was seeing correctly. There was a rope strung across the Rift. *Great. Here we go.*

On the eastern side, a person was sitting on one of the concrete barriers. Somehow he'd already made it across. *Pretty bold of someone to try crossing at a viewpoint. Judgment will probably be hard against whoever this person is.*

He left his lights and siren off. He wanted a closer look and worried the perpetrators would panic. Besides, the SBS&R was already there. *They must have a handle on the situation.*

Arcon struggled to snake the paracord up and over each pole. He had to rest after each loop. Eventually he got his hands on the super-rope and wrapped it twice around one of the reflector poles. "I got it attached," he said. "But I need to secure it better."

Elaina watched him fuss with the rope. She looked around at the small crowd. Her heart stopped. An SUV was approaching with a rack of lights on top. *A Rift ranger.*

Elaina was concerned for her dad. He wasn't acting in an official capacity today and shouldn't have flashed his badge around. She tapped him on the shoulder and pointed toward the vehicle. He shook his head and walked over to meet the new arrival.

She heard Arcon say, "I'm secure now on this side."

"Hold tight for a moment," said Elaina. "We have an issue over here."

CHAPTER TWENTY-FOUR

Ranger Dan drove past the cluster of onlookers and parked near the rescue vehicle. As he climbed out, one of the rescuers approached. "What have you got going on here?"

"There's someone on the other side we're trying to help," said Roberto.

"Okay. How did he get over there?"

Roberto turned away, looked across the Rift, then back at the ranger. "That's a hard question to answer."

Dan waited for more of a response but it didn't come. "Is that your rope across there, or is it his?"

"Uhh, it's mine. Well, it belongs to SBS&R."

The rescuer was acting nervous. Dan wondered why. "Is there something you're not telling me?"

The rescuer looked at the ground, then at the crowd of people watching them. He stepped closer to Dan, and in a whispered voice confided, "He's one of the Mojave People."

"He's what?" exclaimed Dan.

Roberto eyed the crowd again. "I think you'll agree we need to keep this quiet. You're the authority for this area, right?"

"That's correct."

Roberto coaxed Dan to take a few more steps away from the others. "The young man is one of the Mojave People. He's asked us to help him get out of that area. We agreed to do that."

171

"SBS&R should have informed me first."

"I know, and I apologize, but this isn't an *official* rescue."

"You're acting on your own? But you're in uniform."

"It's not right, and I know it. But right now we need to finish this operation. Once he gets to this side, I'll turn him over to you. But he may be in danger where he is now. We need to act fast."

"I guess I understand. That means a rescue drone is out of the question. That'd take hours."

"We have a plan in place that should work, but we could use your help."

"Okay, but even though this isn't official, I expect you to know your job."

"I'll take full responsibility."

"Right. Let me make a call first, and then I'll help however I can. And take off that shirt and badge!"

"Fine," said Roberto. "I'll let my daughter know what's happening."

"Daughter?"

"Yeah, daughter. She's a rescuer too, but, uhh—"

"What is it?"

"To be honest, she's been communicating with this man for years."

"You're kidding. You know that's not right."

"We know," said Roberto, as he turned to look at Elaina. "I need to ask a big favor of you, as the authority here."

"What's that?"

"She's wanted to meet this young man for years. Could you give them a little time together? Supervised, of course. Maybe a couple hours?"

Dan looked at the girl standing on the edge of the Rift. "I'll give them an hour at most. Then I must give him a debriefing of my own."

"Great. I'll let her know."

Ranger Dan went back to his SUV and got in. He tapped his shoulder phone and said, "Call Becca."

"Rift Ranger Station, this is Ranger Becca. How can I help you?"

"Hi Becca. I've got a situation down here at the Freeway Viewpoint."

"Whatcha got?"

"Someone trying to cross the Rift again."

"Are they in danger? Do you need support?"

"There are some SBS&R folks here, so I think we're fine. But there's another issue."

"What's that?"

"There are unconfirmed reports that this person may be one of the Mojave People."

"Oh." Dan heard silence for a moment. "How do you want me to handle that?" asked Becca.

"Contact Regional. Let them know about the situation. Tell them the reports are in question, and I'll get back to them as soon as I know more. Can you do one more thing?"

"Sure. What is it?"

"We have several onlookers down here. Could you monitor the scanners for any unusual activity? Query the searchnet for CalNeva Rift news. Keep me informed."

"Got it Dan. God be with you."

"Thanks, Becca."

Elaina chewed her nails, waiting while her dad spoke with the Ranger The Ranger got back into his vehicle and appeared to be making a call. That can't be good. Arcon was pacing on the other side. "Just rest a little longer," she said, as her dad came walking back.

"Well, I have good news and bad news," said Roberto. "I had to tell the ranger the whole story. Who Arcon is, where he's from, the works."

"Daaaad!"

"Girl, it's okay. The ranger sympathizes with what we're trying to do. He's not real happy, but has agreed to help us anyway he can."

"Okay. Keeping all those people back would be a good start."

"He'll handle the crowd. We discussed a rescue drone, but agreed there was too much red tape and too little time. I've agreed to take responsibility for any accidents that might occur."

"Was that the bad news?"

"No. The bad news is, when Arcon arrives, the ranger wants him at the station for debriefing."

"Oh no, Dad, we wanted to avoid that."

"It can't be helped. But—"

"But what?"

"He's agreed not to take him away immediately. He'll give you two some time. Maybe an hour."

"Oh, Daddy," she said, crying. "Thank you so much."

"Thank the ranger ... later. Let's get that young man over here!"

"Gladly," she said. "Arcon, we're ready on our side. What do you need us to do?"

"I need the super-rope as tight as possible."

Roberto narrowed his eyes, remembering how Arcon had moved in the trees. "Why?" he asked, dreading Arcon's answer.

"I'm going to run the rope."

Roberto reached over and muted the base. "I was afraid he'd say that."

"Oh no," said Elaina.

Roberto walked over to the super-rope, to the edge of the freeway section, then back to his vehicle. "I need to talk to the ranger," he said. "Monitor the kid."

Elaina watched her dad and the ranger. She turned and saw Arcon pacing again. She wished she could see what the future held. She softly prayed for wisdom and safety for everyone involved. Her dad walked up behind her, put his arm over her shoulder, and joined her in prayer.

Roberto took the base from Elaina, unmuted it, and said, "Arcon, listen to me carefully."

"I'm listening," came the reply.

"One rope by itself can hold your weight so we're good there. But we had to tie two lengths together to make it long enough, so you'll run into the knots. Got that? A total of three knots all together."

"I understand."

"These ropes will stretch, so we'll need to make it tight so it doesn't sag. I'll pull my vehicle forward to stretch it tight. But if I pull too hard, the rope could snap violently. If you're close to it, it could take your leg off. Do you understand?"

"I should stay away until you have it tight."

"Exactly. Do you have it tied down securely on your end?"

"Yes."

"Then step away. I'll try to tighten it." Roberto told Elaina to step back and signaled to the ranger to get the crowd at a safe distance. When everything was ready, he put his vehicle in gear and pulled forward. Elaina signaled when the rope straightened out. Roberto set the brake and shut off his rig.

After cautiously testing how taut the rope was with his hands, he told Arcon to try standing on it, warning him to be over the freeway when he did so. Arcon stood on the barricade and pressed down on the rope with one foot, then put his full weight on it. "Can you get it a little tighter?"

"I'll try," said Roberto. He pulled a little harder with the SRV until he was afraid the ropes would snap. Then he signaled to Arcon who tested it again.

"It's like a weak branch, but I think I can do it."

Arcon studied the scene. Something was missing. At ArcPoint, there were many places where they had tied a rope between two trees like this, but those runs were short. In the trees, when he'd run the branches there were other branches around to steady him, or to grab if he fell. He rarely used them, but had never gone without them. Here, there was nothing but open air.

He slowly walked on the rope towards the Rift and his legs went stiff with fear. He unconsciously grabbed for a branch that wasn't there and fell off the rope to the pavement.

"Arcon, wait!" Roberto said in his ear. "Don't start walking this way yet!"

"I wasn't," responded Arcon, "I was just testing things." He didn't want to tell them he was losing his nerve.

"I have two tricks for you," said Roberto. "First, can you find something you can use as a pole—you know, like a stick or a branch?"

Arcon looked around but didn't see any on the ground. He didn't want to go back to the trees to get one. Then he saw a tree on the opposite side of the I-15. "I can get one."

"Fine. Get one at least as long as you are tall. Not too heavy because you'll need to carry it with you."

Arcon thought about that. *I get it. A branch to steady me.* He searched until he found a suitable branch and hacked it off the tree. He sheared the branches where his hands would go so it felt balanced. "Got it," he announced.

"Great," said Roberto. "Now, take your knife and cut off a piece of the small rope about four meters, uh, make it fifteen feet long."

After doing that, he said, "Got it."

"Great. Now, can you tie a bowline? It's like a loop in a rope that won't tighten."

"We call it a goat knot."

Roberto thought about that. "Right, so it won't strangle them."

"Uh-huh."

"Okay, tie a big bowline around your waist with the other end hanging behind you like a dog's tail."

Arcon did as he was told and said, "Got it."

"Now, when you're ready, get on the super-rope and tie the other end of the rope to it with another bowline … er, goat knot.

That way, if you slip, the small rope will catch you. As you walk, it will just slide along the super-rope behind you."

"I get it!" exclaimed Arcon. "The small rope will catch me if I fall, and the branch will help me balance."

"Exactly. Practice with the branch before you start over the Rift. Let us know when you're ready."

"I'll do that. Thank you, Mr. Roberto. Love you." He thought he heard Elaina laugh, and then there was a sudden silence in his ear.

He practiced, walking back and forth on the super-rope, feeling more and more confident. He no longer had the fear that had caused him to stiffen up.

He practiced for a half hour, walking back and forth, from the barricade to the edge of the Rift. He had only fallen twice—once when he turned around, and once when he tripped over the rope attached to his back. He overcompensated with the branch at first, but learned quickly. Then he said, "I'm ready to go now. Pray for me."

He listened as Roberto and Elaina prayed. His confidence rose, boosted to another level, not only to accomplish the task, but to even make the attempt. Arcon took a deep breath, exhaled, and started walking.

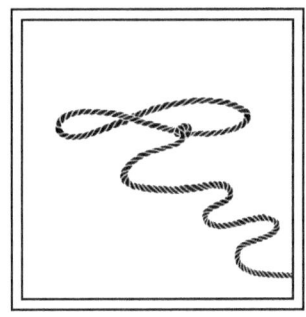

CHAPTER TWENTY-FIVE

Arcon moved swiftly until he first stepped over the abyss, then his legs locked with fear when his peripheral vision saw nothing but air. He willed himself to remember the safety rope and the prayers. He edged forward, picking up speed as he went.

One foot after the other, he was soon halfway across the Rift. He reached the first knot in the rope assembly and stepped gingerly over it. But his safety rope snagged and jerked him off-balance. He fell backward, caught himself, and had to swing the stick wildly to stay upright. Then he had to wait until both the rope and his heart calmed down.

He slowly reversed until he could see the knot and slip the loop over with his foot. He located the others and did the same as he progressed.

The rope appeared to be stretching and sagging more. The approach to the other side was getting steeper. He felt his moccasins starting to slide, so he stopped. He inched forward, making it a few more feet before his foot slipped again. "I'm stuck," he said, hoping they were listening.

"What's the problem," said Roberto. "Is it too steep?"

"Yes," said Arcon. "No foot grip."

"Hold on, don't move. We'll see if we can tighten the ropes." As Ranger Dan approached, Roberto said to him, "The rope is too loose. I need to move the SRV forward to tighten it."

Dan walked to the edge of the Rift and scrutinized Arcon's predicament. "I wouldn't move the vehicle if I were you. Any sudden movement could shake him off the rope." Arcon was close to ten meters from the edge, but was still too far to reach. They couldn't repel down because he was out, not down.

"What are you using for a safety rope?" asked Ranger Dan.

"Standard paracord. It's all we had," said Roberto.

"That's not good. It's typically five hundred pound test, and he could weigh half that. If he falls, the sudden pull could snap it."

"Could he drop down and try to pull himself up the rope?" asked Roberto.

Dan snapped his finger. "Wait, I have a better idea. I can do this."

"Do what?"

Ranger Dan dug a rope out from the back of his vehicle. "Lasso him."

"Like a cow?"

"Just like a cow," he said, as he made a loop in the rope. "Even easier. He's not moving."

"Are you sure?"

"I used to compete in the rodeo in my younger days. If he can stay on that rope a bit longer, I can do it."

Waiting was making Arcon nervous. His legs were knotting up from balancing himself. "Arcon, can you hear me," asked Roberto.

"Yes, please hurry," he said.

"We're going to throw a rope around you. Don't try to catch it! Just hold still."

"Okay, not moving." He couldn't see anybody at first because he was too low. Then a stranger appeared at the edge and swung a coil of rope over his head. It flew and landed around Arcon's neck like a goat rope. The weight pulled him forward; he dropped to a crouch to keep from falling.

"That was a close one," said Roberto. "Now, if you can, get the rope under your armpits." Arcon's whole body shook as he took one hand off the branch and put that arm through the rope, then the other. "That's good, Arcon, we've got you now. Try to move up the rope while we pull on you."

Inching along, Arcon made it half the distance when both feet slid down and out from under him. He fell forward, using the branch to protect his face from the super-rope. He landed off center when he hit the rope and bounced away too quickly to grab it.

He felt a jerk on his mid-section. Just as abruptly, it left, replaced by a pain in his armpits. His headfirst tumble reversed and the rope under his arms appeared in front of him. He grabbed as high as he could and pulled.

Arcon flew through the air, the rope tight under his armpits, and the side of the Rift racing towards him. He instinctively buried his face in his arms as his body slammed into the canyon wall.

Pain shot through his left arm and he lost his grip. He grabbed again with his right; his left wasn't much use. He heard screaming and voices but not from the earpiece. He'd lost it during the impact.

Elaina screamed when Arcon disappeared beneath the freeway's edge. "Oh no God, please no, please no!"

Ranger Dan gripped the rope and yelled, "He's still there! Tie it off, quick. I can't hold it!"

Roberto grabbed ahold and yelled, "It's too short." He pulled, straining to help Dan. "Girl, get over here!"

Elaina wedged in, planted her feet, and pulled. "Arcon, can you hear me? Are you all right?" She heard nothing in her earpiece. "Arcon, are you there?" Still nothing.

All three pulled but the rope wasn't moving. Roberto yelled, "On the count of three, pull! One, two three!"

With each pull, the rope rose a few inches. "Dad, I'm not hearing anything from Arcon. Can you two hold it by yourself?"

"Let's try it," said Roberto. "Let go slowly."

Elaina let go. The rope dropped a little, and the other two leaned into it. "Go ahead," said Ranger Dan. "Check him out."

As Elaina headed toward the edge, her dad shouted, "Girl! Get roped up! I don't want you leaning over that chasm without protection."

"Ahhhh," Elaina protested, then ran for the SRV. In a few minutes, she came back wearing a climbing harness and dragging a rope. She snaked one end through her rescue belay and attached it to the SRV. "Ready."

"Let me clear you," said Roberto.

Elaina walked over to him so he could inspect her gear. "What do you want me to do?"

"See if you can reach him," said Roberto. If you can pull on him, maybe we can get him on top."

Elaina fed line through the belay as she moved to the edge of the cliff. Leaning over the edge she yelled, "Arcon, are you okay?"

He looked up at her. "I can't use my left arm."

"Try to reach me with your right." She laid down on top of the cliff and held out her hand. He reached for it, but fell short.

She stood back up and yelled, "Dad, it's too far. I have to go down."

"Okay," said Roberto. "Hold on." He thought for a moment. "Rappel down until you're under him, then try pushing him up to take the weight off of us. Once we're resituated, we'll have you push him up as we pull."

"How about if I use a foot ascender?"

"Great idea."

Elaina ran to get the ascender, attached it to her foot, and went back to the edge. She looked at her dad, tapped her ear, and said, "Can you hear me in your earpiece?"

"Loud and clear."

"Roger that," she said. "Going down."

As she stepped over the edge of the cliff, she saw Arcon's eyes get big. "Don't worry, I know what I'm doing. Trust me."

In a trembling voice he said, "I trust you."

She rappelled past him, moved sideways until she was under him, and worked the rope into the ascender. She tested it, then yelled, "Arcon!"

"I'm here," he replied.

"I know that," she said under her breath. "Put your feet on my shoulders!"

"Are you sure?"

"Yes! Just do it!" She pulled her leg with the ascender up, while grabbing Arcon's feet with her hands. When she got positioned, she said, "Bend your legs as I stand up." When he did, she stood until her legs were locked. "Now try standing up. Dad, you should get some slack."

As Arcon stood, she heard her dad say, "Got it. Hold there for a minute."

"We're good." Then she asked Arcon, "Are you okay to stand there for a while?"

"I'm good if you are."

"I'm fine. Try to stay still."

After a few minutes, she heard Roberto say, "We're ready to pull again. Tell Arcon to watch his fingers."

"Roger that. Arcon, they're going to pull you up. I'll move up under you like we did before. When you're ready to stand, they'll pull. Watch your fingers so they don't get crushed between the rope and the rock."

"I agree to your terms," said Arcon, as he pulled his arm down and grabbed the rope closer to his chest. "Is this okay?"

"That'll work." Elaina moved up the rope again while Arcon crouched on her shoulders. When they were ready, she said, "Okay guys, one, two, three, *PULL.*"

The rope slid up and Elaina yelled, "We're almost there. I'll get positioned for one more push, and you should be able to grab him."

Elaina moved up the rope again, this time as far as she could go. When Arcon was ready, she said. "Once more guys. One, two, three, *PULL.*"

"I see him," yelled Roberto.

"I've got his weight," said Elaina.

"Grab him," said Dan, "I've got the rope."

Roberto reached down as Arcon reached up and they grabbed each other's wrists. In a sudden jerk, Arcon's belly hit the pavement. Elaina pushed his legs up and Arcon rolled himself over and lay gasping, flat on his back.

Elaina scrambled over the edge of the cliff and crawled to him. Putting her hand on his leg, she said, "You can rest now."

He tried to get to his feet, but collapsed. Ranger Dan said to Elaina, "He flew into that cliff pretty hard."

Arcon flopped his head back to the ground, stared up at the sky and said, "Tweet, tweet."

CHAPTER TWENTY-SIX

A large man reached down, offering to help Arcon to his feet. Arcon was dead tired and dazed as he brought the man in uniform into focus. "Are you Roberto?"

The Ranger laughed and helped him up. "No, son. That would be the man over there, staring at his rope draped across the Rift. I think he's trying to figure out how he'll get it back. I'm Ranger Dan."

Arcon rubbed at his face. Taking a stab at humor, he looked to his left and said, "You must be Elaina."

She tilted her head and gave him a funny look. "Well, by a process of elimination, you got that right."

He hoped for a laugh. With no clue how to formally greet her, he resorted to some of Jarden's advice. "An old friend told me, when I saw you, I should tell you something. He said you'd probably know what it means. I don't."

"What is it?.

Arcon straightened and said, "Me, Tarzan. You, Jane."

Elaina and Ranger Dan burst into laughter. "Boy, you got that right!" said Dan, looking him up and down. "You are a sight!" He saw blood dripping from Arcon's hand. "Looks like you could use some medical attention."

"I'm all out of skin patches."

Elaina saw Arcon was cradling his left arm. "How about your arm? It's not broken, is it?"

He stretched it out. Wincing, he said, "It's still working. Sure hurts though. So does my left hip."

Ranger Dan turned to Elaina. "I know I promised you two some time together, but how about we get him to the station and tend to these injuries? Some of this looks pretty bad."

"Can I talk to my dad about it? He doesn't like me making medical decisions during a rescue."

"Sure, no problem," said the ranger. "I'll see if I can disperse the crowd."

When the ranger walked away, Elaina helped Arcon over to Roberto, who was rummaging around in his vehicle. Before she could speak, Roberto grabbed Arcon and turned him around. "Let me see something." He grabbed the piece of paracord still attached to Arcon's waist and examined it. "Arcon, this rope has been damaged. That's why it broke when you slipped."

Elaina's eyes widened. Her hand went to her mouth. "It broke?"

"See where it frayed? It was sliced by something," said Roberto.

Arcon pulled a face. "That was me. I started to cut it to my height, then remembered you wanted it longer. I didn't know I'd damaged it."

"If we hadn't lassoed you, you'd have fallen to the bottom of the Rift. Arcon, you owe that ranger your life."

Arcon hugged himself. "I need to go thank him." He started walking that direction.

Elaina grabbed his arm. "Whoa, whoa, whoa, Tarzan. You better wait till he disperses the crowd. You're not quite dressed for public appearances yet."

Roberto laughed. "Tarzan. I like that. Are you Jane?"

"It appears I am," said Elaina.

"I still don't understand," said Arcon.

Elaina laughed. "Later. Anyway, Dad, the ranger wants to take Arcon to the station to look at these wounds. I'd like us to go along."

Roberto examined Arcon's hands. There was very little fresh blood. "I'd like to get my ropes back first. I think if I pull it with the right timing, I can get it swinging."

"Like a jump rope?" asked Elaina.

"Right. I think those poles will bend over if I get the rope to ride high enough. If that doesn't work, I'll have to cut it loose on this side. Then there'll be questions about how it got there."

"Okay. I'll go tell the ranger. Pulling on the rope will give him a good excuse to get the crowd at a safe distance."

"Exactly. I'll signal you when I'm ready to try pulling."

Elaina led Arcon to the SRV and gave him her dad's shirt. "Here, put this on so you look more normal." Then she ran off to talk to the ranger. It was too small, so he wore it like a blanket.

Roberto climbed into the SRV and pushed open the passenger door. "Hop in." Arcon climbed into the seat. Roberto showed him how to secure a strap around his waist. Then he looked over, saw the ranger near a crowd, and Elaina pointing a thumb up at the sky.

Arcon watched closely as Roberto started the vehicle. He felt it rumble and purr. He'd always been fascinated by the concept of driving, and now he finally got to watch it happen. There were things to step on and levers to pull. He could hear the engine speed up and slow down, while the vehicle lurched back and forth.

He knew he'd tied the rope securely, so he didn't think this machine could pull it away. His eyes darted, watching Roberto's movements, watching the ropes, listening to the engine whine.

Roberto started a rhythmic tugging, and the rope arched higher and higher into the air. He suddenly stepped hard on the floor pedal, and the vehicle lurched forward. Roberto stepped on another pedal and the vehicle jerked to a stop. Arcon looked back. Two of the metal poles were missing, and so was the rope. Roberto drove forward and dragged most of it onto the pavement.

Elaina ran to help her dad with the ropes. She stopped and told Arcon, "Stay in here." He'd already been told that by Roberto and wondered why it was so important.

He watched the handful of people in the distance. Some of them would tap something on their shoulders occasionally, but he didn't know why. He waited patiently while the other two struggled with the super-rope and finally got it in the vehicle.

Roberto hopped back in with Arcon. "We're going to the ranger station, so they can look at those cuts on your hands and get you something to drink. Elaina will follow in her three-wheeler." Roberto handed him a brown coat. "Cover yourself. We don't need paparazzi following us."

Arcon did not understand who Papa Rotsy was but trusted Roberto. He hid himself under the coat. He watched Elaina get into a small vehicle. Then he felt a strange sensation as the one he was in picked up speed over the land.

This was faster than he'd ever flown through the trees. He could see far into the distance without having to climb. All without leaving his seat. Roberto made it all happen while barely moving. Arcon was nervous, but so far the outside world was thrilling.

Roberto drove down the highway and into the hills until they came to a cluster of buildings. People were meandering around, crossing the street. "This is Calico. You said you knew about this town."

"Not this," said Arcon. "I only know about the *windows* of Calico." He paused as the town rolled by. "The windows of heaven," he mumbled.

Roberto looked over at Arcon, who appeared lost in thought. Whatever he'd meant by "heaven" could be discovered later.

Roberto pulled into the parking lot of the ranger station. "Here we are." Arcon looked like he was in a daze. "Don't worry, these are good people. They'll have a lot of questions." That statement didn't seem to get Arcon's attention, so he added, "They may be the authority here, but Jesus is the ultimate authority."

Arcon's eyes widened. He sat up straight in his seat. "Is Jesus ruling from Jerusalem?"

Surprised by the response, Roberto asked, "Do you know about Jesus?"

"I'm not sure how much I know," said Arcon. "My grandma talked about Him a lot. She said someday he'd return and rule from a far away place called Jerusalem. But before then, he'll gather all his people in the sky to meet him, and that includes the ArcPoint people." They sat silent for a moment. Arcon mumbled, "Maybe she was wrong."

"She was right about some of it," said Roberto. "From what I've heard about the time when Jesus returned, everybody was wrong in one way or another. But those who knew Him within recognized Him immediately."

"That's how I know Him, in here, inside me. I don't know how to explain it, but He helps me, guides me, encourages me to take wise risks."

"Like walking across a canyon?"

"Exactly. Some would say it was unwise, not worth the risk. But I believe Jesus is watching me, somehow knowing what's ahead of me, and how I should get there."

He looked out the window and saw Elaina drive past in her strangely familiar vehicle. "Mr. Roberto, I believe it was Jesus who put the desire in my heart to leave the ArcPoint Community, to risk traveling to this unknown place. He allowed me to see Elaina without my eyes and never lose sight of her. Does any of that make sense?"

"Makes perfect sense," said Roberto. "I can't wait to hear more. But let's get this ranger business out of the way first. Besides, Elaina's eager to spend some quiet time with you."

Elaina knocked on Arcon's window and smiled at him.

"I've never had quiet time *with* someone," replied Arcon, as he tried to figure out how the door could be opened.

Elaina opened it for him. "What were you two talking about?"

Arcon said, "Quiet."

She frowned and whispered, "Oh, okay. Sorry."

"Arcon meant the quiet of the forest," said Roberto. He's looking forward to some quiet time with you."

"Oh, me too," said Elaina. "I'll try not to talk your ear off, but I can't wait for us to share our lives. I mean, you know, share stories about growing up in our own little worlds."

"Your world is not little," said Arcon, as he got out of the car and glanced around. "But I know what you mean." He looked at the building they were standing next to. "I grew up in a house made out of trees like this one. We called it a log cabin. It wasn't this big."

"We call them log cabins too," said Elaina. "We finally have something in common."

"It's certainly not the wardrobe," mumbled Roberto.

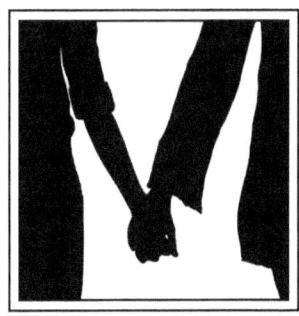

CHAPTER TWENTY-SEVEN

In the ranger station a woman in uniform with a slight build and a beaming smile met them. "You must be Tarzan," she said with a laugh. "Ranger Dan told me about you. He'll be here soon. Let's go look at those wounds." She turned to Elaina and Roberto. "Would either of you care to join us?"

Elaina said, "Dad, maybe you should help Arcon. I'll wait here."

"That's probably wise. I'll just follow ranger, uh—"

"Becca," said the lady ranger, "Becca White." She turned to Elaina. "I have the inter-agency forms on the counter there. You can start filling those out. Take your time, it may be awhile."

Roberto gave his daughter a look of regret, but she acknowledged, with a flick of her fingers, that he should move along. He was glad they understood one another. He usually filled out the paperwork for a rescue, especially when two agencies worked together on it. But he didn't want any paperwork on this operation. He'd have to deal with that later.

It'd been years since Roberto had been in this ranger station. Not since he and Elaina had first heard Arcon's communications. They'd come to talk with the authority ranger about the rules for crossing into the restricted Mojave area.

He was glad a new person was in that role, remembering how strict the former Authority had been. But it had worked to scare Elaina away from using the scanner, temporarily.

He'd avoided this place; afraid his child would blurt out something about Arcon that would get him in hot water. These rangers seemed more reasonable.

Ranger Becca led them to a meeting room and had Arcon rest his arm on a table. Roberto slid a chair closer. She searched his leather arm coverings, trying to find the end of the leather strings holding them on.

"Under here," said Arcon. He rolled his arm to one side and tugged at the strings.

"Okay, I get it. They're tucked in. Let me take care of that for you."

"I usually loosen it and pull."

"I think I'll unlace it all the way." As she worked her way up his arm, she asked, "Does this have fur on the inside?"

"Yes, rabbit fur. It keeps the thorns farther from the skin. Wears better that way too."

"Okay, well, we'll certainly need some antiseptic." She peeled one of them open. "This fur is caked with blood."

"Sorry about that, ma'am. I don't mean to upset you."

"No, that's okay. Doesn't it hurt?"

"Well, yeah, but right now it itches more than it hurts."

"I don't want you to scratch it. That may infect it. I'll give you something for the itching." She peeled the fur away from his arm as delicately as she could. "What is this stuff covering the cuts?"

"Skin patches. I didn't have enough."

"What are they made of?"

"Well, mostly bark from the ArcPoint trees, but the chemists put other stuff in it."

"He's talking about the acacia trees," added Roberto. He looked closer. "Looks like paper."

"It is," said Arcon. "A specially treated paper made just for skin patches. It takes the pain away faster than anything else."

"Fascinating," said Becca. "So you make your own paper?"

"We make everything we need. We have to. What is that stuff you're using?"

"It's just some alcohol for cleaning around the wounds. Did they have alcohol where you come from?" she asked, dabbing at each puncture wound.

"Sure. We used alcohol to clean with too, and burned it in lamps. We used it for a lot of things."

Arcon's countenance changed. His chin quivered. Ranger Becca asked, "What's the matter?"

Arcon didn't respond for a moment. "It was my parent's job to make alcohol for our community. Something went wrong and there was an explosion. They didn't survive."

"Oh, I'm sorry to hear that. How awful for you."

"That's okay, ma'am, but I'd rather not talk about it."

"Sure, I understand."

Roberto watched as Becca cleaned away the last of the blood. Then she looked closely at Arcon's arm and her eyes went big. She turned away, said, "Wait here, I need to get something," and dashed out of the room.

Roberto said, "Arcon, I'll go check on Elaina, okay?"

"Sure, I'll stay here."

Roberto left, but instead of going to Elaina, he tracked down Ranger Becca. "Are you okay?"

"Did you see those scars on his arms?" she asked. "Hundreds of them. A lot of them from when he was very young. What kind of people are we dealing with here?"

"Now, calm down. We're not sure yet what the people are like over there, but we've seen no evil in this young man."

"But how do we know? I know what Ranger Dan told me, but this young man should really be at a Containment Center."

"I understand your concern," he said. "But at the moment none of these medical issues are life threatening. If there are some issues with his past, we can deal with that later. I just ask that you help him now."

"How long have you known him?"

"Well, we just recently met, but we've communicated with him for over eight years. He's given us no sign of an evil nature in all that time."

"I'm sorry, you're right," she said. "None of what I see is serious. Nothing requires stitches, and he seems polite. There are just so many scars. I wish I knew how he got them."

"Why don't you ask? Or are you afraid to be in the room with him?"

"No, no. I'll be okay."

"Thanks for understanding. I need to check on my daughter. I'll be right back."

Ranger Becca grabbed an extra first aid kit and Roberto went to the front to see Elaina, who was talking with the ranger they'd met at the Rift. "This is Ranger Dan," she said.

"We've met."

"Oh, I know. I just didn't know if you knew his name."

Roberto winked at his daughter. "It's on his name tag." He shook the ranger's hand. "Hey, thanks for helping keep this thing discreet. We have no problem with the news getting out eventually, but we'd like to ease him into this world of ours. You understand."

"Not completely, but I see no reason to rush things. A few of the higher authorities know a little, so we must keep them up to date. As long as there's no indication of a violent nature, I see no need to place him in containment." He turned to Elaina. "I know you'd like to spend some time with him."

"As much as I can get," she said, then blushed realizing how her remark had sounded.

"As long as you give me all your contact information, and keep me informed of his whereabouts, I may consider placing him in your custody."

Roberto shook the ranger's hand again. "It's a deal, thanks. We'll make sure to let you know what he's up to," he said, pointing at the ranger. "Until we get orders to answer to someone else."

"That'll be perfectly fine," said Ranger Dan. "Now let's go back and see how this wild man is doing. I might have something for him. Miss Jane, you may want to stay out here."

"No problem," said Elaina.

Roberto and Ranger Dan returned to find Arcon and Becca talking and laughing. "You actually swing through the trees?" Becca asked, eyes wide. "On a rope?"

"Of course, doesn't everybody?" joked Arcon.

"Hey Dan," said Becca, as they walked in. "Did you know any of this?"

"I knew he was of the Mojave People, but that's all I knew," said Dan.

"Not the Mojave People," said Becca. "It's the Arcpoint Community, uh, what was it … Endeavor! The Arcpoint Community Endeavor. And look at all these scars on his arms! He got these from swinging through the trees!"

"Well," said Arcon, "from swinging badly and falling into the needle brush."

"Needle brush?" asked Dan.

Becca answered, "You know, the stickers that keep springing up over here? The ones we have to spray? Over there they're everywhere. The people can't move around on the ground. They have to swing through the trees to get past them. He got these scars when he fell into the stickers."

"Not all of them," Arcon countered. "We do hack trails through the needle brush, and if we're not careful, we hit the thorns with our arms or hands. That's why we wear skins."

Roberto looked closer. "Some of these scars look old, like you got them as a child."

"Yeah, I got in a lot of trouble for some of those. Children aren't supposed to swing, but I wanted to be like my friend Jarden. I'd sneak into the woods and use the ropes. One time they had to hack quite a bit to get me out of what I fell into.

I was a mess. But the hunters were mostly mad because they had to go back and reset all the ropes I'd messed up."

"So, did the scars come from the thorns or from the punishment?" asked Roberto, glancing at Ranger Becca.

"Nobody needed to punish me for that mistake. The fall was punishment enough."

"Sounds like it," said Ranger Dan. "What did you mean, you had to reset the ropes?"

"Well, the swing-arc has one anchor and two endpoints. You have to start a swing at one endpoint or the other, so you always make sure the rope is waiting for you at the approach, and not dangling in midair." Arcon brightened as he shared the geometry and physics of swing-arc design. He explained how elements of weight and distance determined velocity, and so on.

As the three listened, they nodded knowingly to each other. The Mojave People were presumed to be primitive and timid. This one wasn't.

Roberto eventually interrupted. "We can't wait to hear more, but there's a young lady in the other room, waiting."

"Oh, yes," added Ranger Dan. "But before we let you go, I might have something for you. Follow me, if you're through with him, Becca?"

"I'm finished cleaning the cuts on his arms and hands. Don't know about the rest of him." She asked, "How's your arm doing Arcon? I can see it's starting to bruise up."

"The rest of me is okay," he said, lifting his arm a little. "The arm really hurts, but I can tell it'll be okay, eventually."

"Are you sure you don't need it in a sling?"

"Oh, no. It still works okay."

"Good, then follow me, Tarzan," said Ranger Dan.

Roberto tagged along, wondering what Ranger Dan had in mind. When they got to the station locker room, Ranger Dan looked Arcon up and down. "You're about my height. Not the same around the middle, but that's okay." He opened his locker, grabbed a pair of pants and said, "Here, try these on, see how they fit." He pointed at his own and tugged on their waist.

Arcon held the pants, looked them over, and turned to Roberto, who nodded. Arcon untied his leggings and slipped them off. Then another hide which resembled a Scottish kilt. Under that was what looked like a leather diaper. Then a knitted undergarment that looked like Alpaca wool. Roberto said, "If that's the last layer, you can leave it on."

Arcon grinned at them. "Thanks," he said, and tugged the pants on. He buttoned them at the waist.

"Pull up on that metal tag," advised Ranger Dan. "It's what's called a zipper."

Arcon looked closely, found the tag, and grinned again. The zipper closed, but the pants still wanted to drop. Roberto saw the predicament and removed his own belt and showed Arcon how to weave it through the belt loops and fasten it.

Ranger Dan led him to a full-length mirror. "They're a little baggy, but they look good on you. Now try the shirt."

When Arcon removed his upper hide, they could see how muscular his body was, especially his arms. Many scars peppered his back, along with patches of dried blood.

Before Arcon put on the shirt, Ranger Dan said, "You know, before you put this on, you may want to freshen up." Roberto nodded as Dan led him into the bathroom. "You can shower later when you change those bandages, but for now, use this washcloth to clean up a bit. I suggest cleaning your face *before* you do your armpits."

Arcon looked at him funny and thought about it. Then he lifted one arm and took a sniff. "I understand," he said, and all three laughed.

Roberto cleaned the puncture wounds on Arcon's back. Ranger Dan retrieved one of the first aid kits from Becca so they could bandage those spots to keep his shirt clean.

Arcon said, "Those bandages stick on well, but I think my skin patches feel better."

Roberto nudged Ranger Dan. "They put some sort of chemical in those skin patches to ease the pain. He says they get it from the acacia trees."

"It would be interesting to find out what that chemical is. Arcon, do you have any more of those skin patches?"

"No, sorry. I used them all."

"Can you get more?"

Arcon was silent. Judging by his countenance, neither man felt they should pursue the subject any further.

CHAPTER TWENTY-EIGHT

As Noreena Chan drove into Calico, she sensed a change. When she climbed out of her car, she knew she was right. This was not the same town she'd visited just a few days earlier.

Over the years, as a human-interest reporter, she'd learned to recognize travelers. In big cities, residents rushed from point A to point B, while tourists meandered. In small towns, residents didn't rush and vacationers were nowhere to be seen.

Then there were the tourist towns, where nearly everyone wandering the streets was a traveler, and residents worked the shops. Tourists would walk and gawk more than they talked, and occasionally sit, but rarely ran. And they always huddled around points of interest.

That's how it'd been in Calico days ago, and Fort Irwin as well. But today, everyone in town was talking. She needed to know why. She hoped it wasn't because of a bad accident, which was often the topic of a murmuring crowd.

She stepped onto the boardwalk that snaked its way up the hill in front of the shops. She moved in close behind a couple of women, trying to eavesdrop. They were discussing a rescue near the Rift.

She saw an elderly couple coming, so she turned to stare in a shop window. After they passed, she followed. They were having a discussion about the Mojave People, but that wasn't surprising. The four major attractions to Calico were the Rift, the mining history, the Acacia forest, and as she'd recently discovered, the Mojave People who lived in it.

Noreena went into a small convenience store, hoping to hear what the locals were discussing. She didn't have to wait long. It was a conversation between the shopkeeper and a tourist. Noreena grabbed a jar of locally made jam and joined them at the counter. When there was a lull in the conversation, she said, "Excuse me, did I hear you say something about a Mojave person?"

"You sure did, missy," said a rather animated shopper with a southern drawl. "I seen it with my own two eyes. Some feller wearin' animal skins just tight-roped across the Rift. And not from this side neither. Some rescue folks strung a line over to him and he walked it back. Almost fell in the hole he did. But a big ranger fella lassoed him and pulled him up outta there. Never seen nothin' like it. Heard they took him on up to the ranger station. Don't know for sure though."

"Well, that certainly does sound strange."

"I seen it with my own two eyes," she repeated. "I gotta git back to my husband. Y'all have a nice day."

"You too, ma'am," said Noreena. "Thanks for the information."

Noreena watched the woman walk out of the store. The shopkeeper mumbled, "Sure hope that guy doesn't get away."

"What did you say?" asked Noreena.

"The guy from the Mojave. Hope he doesn't get away. We don't want evil creeping back into our world."

"I don't understand," said Noreena. "I'm not from around here."

"The Mojave People are from the old world, before the return. Don't know where you're from, but I'm sure you understand what those days were like. Evil spirits persuading people to steal, kill, and destroy. Many people think the Mojave is still like that. Still swarming with evil. Don't want that back in our world, no sir."

"Do you think that's true?" asked Noreena, as she set the jam on the counter and peered into the face scanner.

"I don't know for sure," said the shopkeeper. "But I know to be cautious. Around here we keep our eyes open."

"Jesus knows."

"Amen. But don't you think part of our test is obedience? That's why we report anything suspicious. We need to obey the restrictions. I think he tests us to see how we'll react to someone breaking the rules. So, if that man came from the Mojave, he needs to be confined and brought before the judges. We're not to take punishment into our own hands or let evil continue unabated. Where you from, anyway?"

"I just moved to San Bernardino from Oregon. But my heritage is from China."

"Okay … well then … you know how bad we can be with evil spirits driving our thoughts. We don't want any of that from the Devil's Playground."

"Excuse me?"

"That's what they used to call that place. Check the maps prior to the return. You'll see what I mean."

"I'll do that. I'll keep my eyes open."

Roberto looked at the shave Ranger Dan had given Arcon. "That's a definite improvement."

"You don't think I'm being too indulgent, giving him a goatee like mine?"

"Let's ask Ranger Becca," said Roberto.

They walked to where she was putting away the medical supplies and asked in unison, "What do you think, Becca?"

"Wow, looks like Tarzan is ready for New York."

"But what do you think of the goatee?"

"That works. Do you have a comb?"

Roberto reached in his back pocket. "I've got one."

Becca showed Arcon the comb. "You don't mind, do you?"

"No, not if you don't. It's quite a mess."

She looked his tangled hair over. "I think you're right. Do you have anything against pony tails?"

Arcon gave her a contorted grin. "I don't know what you mean."

"Oh, okay. Just a minute." She left the room and came back in with a rubber band. "Trust me with this. If you don't like it we can try something else."

Arcon looked her in the eyes. "I agree to your terms."

Becca chuckled. "What? Oh, okay good. Just hold still." She gathered his long hair and tied it back with the rubber band. "There. Go look in the mirror."

Arcon walked to the mirror and studied his new appearance. "I don't know this person, but I think I like him."

Roberto laughed. "Shall we go see what the boss thinks?"

They found Elaina gazing at the Visitors' monitor. When she looked up, her mouth dropped open. "Hey Dad, who's the new guy?"

"Quite a transformation isn't it? He needs a shower, but we'll wait till we change the bandages."

"At least now he's approachable," joked Ranger Dan.

Roberto caught the look in his daughter's eyes for Ranger Dan's remark. It didn't match her smile. She'd anticipated this meeting for a long time. He'd have been comfortable postponing it indefinitely.

He'd been concerned this whole affair would take a bad turn. She hadn't dated for years. She was pinning too many hopes on this unknown person. But now those concerns were gone. Roberto gave his daughter a quick nod.

She walked over to Arcon. "Can I give you a hug?"

Arcon looked at Roberto, who nodded his approval. Arcon raised his left arm and winced. He wrapped his right arm around Elaina as she wrapped hers around him.

"Welcome to your new world, jungle boy," she said.

Ranger Dan gave Roberto a thumbs-up. "Got a moment?"

"Sure," said Roberto, and followed Ranger Dan into his office.

Inside, Ranger Dan spoke about a debriefing. "One concern of the higher-ups is that this young man may have escaped from that place out of duress. Nobody knows what it's like over there. The theories and rumors run the gamut, but consensus is, Jesus declared that area off-limits for a reason. They fear the evil, common in the former days, is over there. That's why the thorns confine it."

"To be honest, ranger, that was my concern as well. When Elaina first made contact, I wanted her to break it off. She tried to, but felt driven, and I mean God-driven, to communicate with Arcon. It became her ministry. She felt he must be trying to escape, but wasn't evil himself. He made it clear his community would try to stop him from escaping."

"And now?" asked Dan.

"Well, when we began planning his rescue, I didn't know if he was a refugee seeking asylum or a criminal seeking escape. But, already I feel a need to treat him like a son, and not a stranger."

Ranger Dan's eyebrows went up. Roberto shook his head. "Now, don't be putting words in my mouth. I did not say son-in-law. What I'm saying is, I wouldn't be afraid to have him living under my own roof. You know, like an adopted son."

"Even with your daughter there?"

"That creates a complication, but our house is set up. We can make it work. I'll give him my office in the basement. It has its own bathroom. Her room is on the top floor, and mine is on the main. Besides, I trust her."

"But do you trust *him?*"

Roberto thought about that for a while. "I haven't known him long enough… but I do. Somehow I have a peace about it. Plus …" He leaned forward and whispered, "I put a lock on the basement door, just in case."

"That's good enough for me," said Ranger Dan. "I need to assure the authorities he's not a danger to himself or others. If I couldn't, I'd need to incarcerate Arcon until the Judges could determine what to do with him. As Grace and Forgiveness are still the operative rules in our society, I'll recommend we take no action for his crime of leaving the restricted area, and extend him grace to enter our land. Which means, this official debriefing is complete. However, for personal reasons I have a lot of questions for the young man."

"Do you need to ask him now?"

"Now's not a good time. What I recommend is, take him home for a couple days while I work out the details on my end. Let the situation calm down a little. Questioning him now would be like trying to lasso a calf in the midst of a whirlwind."

"I see what you mean."

"Let's figure out how to get him past the people at the gate."

"That's it?" asked Roberto. "He's free to go?"

"I didn't say that," countered Dan. "He's as free as you allow, because I'm putting him in your custody. But honestly, he doesn't appear to be a flight risk. Do you agree?"

"Absolutely. I think he'll stick close to Elaina, and I'll stick close to both of them."

"That's probably wise. He must face the judges at some point, and Jesus will need to bless his permanent freedom. Until then I'll need to track his whereabouts. I expect you to report to me regularly."

Roberto then asked, "What did you mean, people at the gate?"

"There are quite a few rubberneckers who are curious about our guest. I'm sure by now he's the talk of Calico. We'll have to sneak him out of town. Let me make a call."

Dan grabbed the phone, dialed a number, and waited. "Hello Dwight? Can you come back to the office? Good ... Make sure to lock the gate behind you ... I'll explain when you get here ... Right, see you in a few."

Dan disconnected. "Let's go see how the kids are doing."

In the reception area, Elaina was showing Arcon an overhead map of the Mojave forest. Ranger Becca was holding the paperwork Elaina should be filling out.

Dan pulled Becca aside. Roberto talked with Elaina, leaving Arcon to slide his finger around the screen to change the view. When Ranger Dwight arrived, Roberto joined the rangers while Elaina told Arcon what the plan was.

When Elaina was through talking with Arcon, they rejoined the others. "So is it a go?" They all nodded and stood together in prayer, asking God to avert the eyes of the public, at least until this all settled down.

Noreena Chan sat in her car, talking into a voice recorder. "Need to investigate history of Mojave and reasons for restriction." She thought for a moment. "Research crime data before and after return of Jesus." She set the recorder down.

She kept her eyes on the crowd surrounding the locked gate to the ranger station. She'd spoken with several of them, trying not to sound like an investigator. She couldn't help it. Her senses told her there was a story here. A big one. There were certainly differing viewpoints about what took place, but parts of the stories were consistent.

Whoever this fur clad man was, he'd come from the restricted area. How, no one knew.

It involved San Bernardino Search and Rescue. They'd been seen in the area with a drone when a fire was reported. A big man, who'd helped to hold the crowd at bay, had told her for certain they'd used a drone to help the man tightrope across the Rift.

Other than rangers and rescuers, there didn't seem to be anyone else involved. From her vantage point she couldn't see the front parking lot, but assumed everyone had been chased away before it closed. She intended to stay until it reopened and get a glimpse of the man from the Mojave.

"I see him!" yelled someone standing at the gate. "He's walking with the ranger."

The crowd moved closer. Noreena hurried out of her car to join them.

"That's him. They're getting into the ranger's car."

They're moving him. If she couldn't interview this man before he got into the vehicle, she would be there when he got out.

She stood with one hand on the open car door. Gravel crunched behind her. A three-wheeled autocycle with a trailer appeared down the road from the ranger station. *That's the same vehicle I saw the other day. The same girl I talked with is driving. Where did that come from?*

Noreena jumped in her car. The ranger vehicle approached. She edged her car in close behind it. She could see someone in a yellow vest in the back seat. The man driving it was familiar. She smiled, remembering his name. *Ranger Dan Wilson, you said I might want to write a story about you someday. I didn't know it would happen this soon.*

Roberto joined Ranger Becca in opening the gate and watched the crowd scramble to the cars in the roadway. Elaina's three-wheeler disappeared in the distance with no one the wiser. The plan had worked so far. But there were a few stragglers. Becca was responding to their questions.

"Was that one of the Mojave People?" asked one man.

"That has not been officially confirmed at this time," she answered.

"Where are they taking him?" asked another.

"I am not at liberty to divulge that information."

A woman shouted, "Are they taking him someplace secure?"

"As I said, I am not at liberty to divulge that information."

"We saw blood at the viewpoint. Did the cave guy fight with the ranger?"

"He did not. He was not aggressive in any fashion."

When different people asked questions at the same time, Ranger Becca said, "Excuse me, I need to get back to the station. When the time is appropriate, there will be a press release issued. Keep checking the website for further developments."

Roberto walked toward his SRV. He heard footsteps behind him. Turning, he saw the big man he'd put in charge of keeping people away when they'd strung the super-rope.

"Who was the guy you helped across the Rift?" asked the big man.

"I can't really comment on that right now," said Roberto.

"You shook his hand. It looked to me like you knew him."

"I ... I'd never met him before."

"Is he one of the Mojave People?"

"I can't comment on that. It will be up to the authorities and the individual himself to release any information. You understand."

"Yeah, okay. Those people are a mystery. But hey, thanks for letting me help. My dad works at SBS&R too. I know how dangerous your job can be."

"Your dad works where I do?" asked Roberto. "Is he in the field?"

"Naahh, he works in the office. He's an accountant. But I hear stories."

Roberto shook the man's hand. "Well, don't believe everything you hear. Thanks for your help. I need to get going."

"Me too. I'm going to catch the crowd, maybe meet this guy."

"Uhhh ... I think I heard something about Yermo."

"Thanks. I know a shortcut. See ya."

Roberto knew it was only a matter of time before the news spread through the office, but he was prepared to deal with it. Those rumors were like a slow fire compared to the explosion of sparks this story would be if the press were to get involved.

CHAPTER TWENTY-NINE

As Ranger Dan Wilson led the parade of cars through the Calico business district, Noreena saw many people wave at him. When he didn't acknowledge them, their smiles dropped and brows furrowed. That told her Dan's behavior wasn't normal, but not why it wasn't. Was he distracted, moody, or feeling guilty about something?

The locals had told her that every few years, some adventurous person would try to get across the Rift to the other side. So far none had made it before being stopped, usually by Ranger Dan. But this time somebody from that side had come this way, and that had locals spooked. She didn't know why, but they all seemed to think of the Mojave People as crazed wild animals.

The string of cars behind Ranger Dan was growing as he drove toward Yermo. Noreena could see the man in the back seat thrashing around and wondered if he was trying to escape the vehicle. In case he was dangerous, she'd keep her distance.

Elaina checked her mirrors. No one was following her. She was glad they'd split up. Her dad could answer any questions as he checked out of their cabin. They planned to meet at the rest area on the I-15 freeway. By that time they'd be miles away from Ranger Dan and all the drama happening around him.

What will happen when Dan opens the door of his ranger vehicle? So many had followed him, hoping to get a look at the man from the Mojave.

"Can I sit up now?" asked Arcon. "I want to see where you're flying."

"No, you'll have to wait until we get to the freeway. There's a rest area not too far down where I can stop and let you crawl out the back. They have toilets there, too, if you need one. I hope they showed you how to use one at the station."

Arcon scoffed. "We had toilets at ArcPoint. Running water too."

"Oh, sorry," said Elaina. "I didn't mean anything by that. But hey, now we have something else in common."

"I think you'll find we have more in common than you think."

"Such as?"

"Dishes, books, even clothes. I looked strange because I was dressed different. But only the hunters dress like I do. The others wear soft clothes because they don't work in sharp places. We have long-haired goats we shear to make material for clothes. I look more civilized when I'm not hunting."

For the first time she sensed insecurity and frustration from Arcon. It occurred to her that, so far, everyone had been telling him where to sit, what to do, even what clothes to wear. He deserved respect for what he was capable of. "Would you really like to sit up?"

"Yes. It smells bad where my face is. It's probably me. Sorry, I don't mean to offend you. Either way."

She had to smile at his sense of humor. The Mojave People couldn't be as bad as people thought. "Let me find a safe place to pull over and we'll get you out of there. Besides, I don't think anyone will recognize you in those clothes."

She drove a little ways and found a side road and parked behind some trees. She pulled a knob to pop the hatch, then got out and opened it for him. She lifted the towels and spare clothes away.

He twisted and pulled himself out of the small storage area.

Back on solid ground, Arcon stretched to get the kinks out. "Thanks, that's much better."

Elaina flipped the back seat up so he'd have a place to sit, since there was only one seat up front. He crawled in, slouching to fit. "Now I won't miss what's out there," he said, peering out the small window. "There's a lot to see, compared to what I'm used to."

Noreena watched the ranger slow down as he neared a gas station in Yermo. Assuming he was stopping for gas, she pulled off the road just before, so she'd be ready when he left. But he drove past the station and into a restaurant parking lot. All the cars behind followed him in, before she could get back on the road. She had to park a block away from the restaurant. By the time she got to the front door, people were getting into their cars to leave. She wondered why.

Inside the restaurant, two rangers were in the far corner, but no one wearing animal skins or an orange vest. She scurried out the door and spotted the big man she'd talked to earlier. She stopped him as he was leaving. "Remember talking to me up at the ranger station earlier?"

"You asked me about the Mojave man."

"Yes. Did you see him when he got here?"

He laughed. "Old Ranger Dan got us good with that one. He dressed Ranger Dwight up in a caveman suit and fooled us all. The Mojave guy musta got snuck out with someone else. 'Spose you could try back at the station, but I bet they whisked him off somewhere. Good luck."

"He went with the rescue people?"

"I wouldn't think so, but I could find out. My dad works for them."

"Really? Can I get his contact info?"

"It won't help you now. He's not working today so he won't know this even happened."

"Okay. Here's my contact number, anyway. I work for the Portal and would like to do a story about this man. I'd appreciate if you could call your dad. Have him contact me if he finds out anything."

"Sure, I'll do that. Here's my number too, just in case you find out what's going on. It's mighty mysterious. Maybe try back at the station, see if he's still there."

"I may do that. Thanks for your help."

As the man drove away, she considered going inside to question the rangers. But she didn't enjoy being the butt of a joke. Taking the man's advice, she headed back to the ranger station.

For years, Elaina had wished for real time with Arcon. She'd dreamed of a conversation without the limitations of archaic technology. Now that they were alone, they were strangely silent.

From her perspective, Arcon only commented about what he saw out the window and how it compared to where he came from. The vast open landscape was free of ArcPoint trees and needle brush. The expanse of the sky was broad, not narrow like over the facility, and not filtered through the branches. He could see large hills in the distance, while in the forest they wouldn't see a hill until they were climbing it. He thought driving had to be the best sport there was. She was ready to pounce on any question he had about her, but one never came.

She knew he must be hungry; she was. "Shall we hit a drive-through on the way home?"

There was no response. Eventually Arcon said, "I don't know what you mean."

"A fast-food restaurant? Are you hungry?"

"Yes. The candy things at the ranger station didn't last."

"What do you like to eat?"

"Spaghetti."

"Oh, so do I, but I want to stop somewhere we can stay in the car. Just trust me. I'll order for both of us."

"I trust you."

"What did you say this was?" asked Arcon.

Elaina swallowed what she was eating. "It's a burrito. And those crispy things are French fried potatoes."

"We had potatoes, but never like these."

"How do you like the coffee?"

"It's a lot stronger than Grandma's herbal tea."

"You should have tried a soft drink."

"How can a drink be soft?"

"To be honest, I don't know why they call them that. Are you ready for dessert?"

"I like desserts."

"You liked chocolate. I'll get you a chocolate sundae."

"Then I'm glad today is Sunday."

Elaina just smiled, started her car, and got back in line at the drive-thru window.

"Excuse me. Were you one of the people who helped rescue the Mojave man?"

Roberto turned. A small-framed woman with Asian features and dark reddish hair was talking to him. He knew he couldn't lie, so he tried to change the subject. "Why do you ask?"

"I'm a reporter for the *San Bernardino Portal*. I think it's important for people in our area to know what happened. Were you there?"

"I'm not really at liberty to discuss the operation."

"Then who is? Should I talk to the rangers?"

"They are the authorities for this area."

"Does that include the Mojave Forest?"

"You'll have to ask them, ma'am. Sorry, I need to be going."

"You do realize the Mojave is a restricted area, that violating those rules requires incarceration, and that incarcerations are public knowledge?"

"No comment," said Roberto.

"Fine then. I have connections at the SBS&R so I'll get the information some other way. Just be informed that I'll want to interview you regarding this. I always get my facts straight and that requires an eyewitness if possible. I believe you are that person. I believe I can find out where you live."

Her boldness shocked him. "Someday I'll grant you that interview, but I can't comment at this time. Please excuse me."

Now he regretted returning to the station. He'd hoped to give Ranger Dan his personal ID code so they could communicate securely. He hadn't counted on running into a reporter.

He scribbled the code on a piece of paper and handed it to Ranger Becca. "See that Ranger Dan gets this." Then he whispered, "And make sure that reporter doesn't see it."

Noreena tapped Roberto on the shoulder. "Excuse me? I'm only trying to do my job. Secrecy and anonymity were once used to destroy our world. Now we trust others, and we trust our Lord. I'd just like to gather the facts while I'm on the scene, that's all."

"I apologize. I'm sure you can be trusted, ma'am. But now is just not the time, and I'm not the person. Give your information to the rangers and you'll be the first reporter they contact. Sorry, I need to leave."

CHAPTER THIRTY

"Were you involved with the rescue at the freeway viewpoint?" asked a gray-haired man.

This was the second stranger to ask Roberto that question since he'd come to the rest area. "I can't comment on anything regarding the operation at the Rift," he said.

"Do the rangers know something?"

"I wouldn't bother them."

"Why not?"

"The Mojave is a restricted area, so anything regarding that area is also restricted, until the authorities deal with it. Put a query in your search-net device and wait for official information. That's all I can say about it. Sorry."

Roberto just wanted to get home to be with Elaina. She may be twenty-one, but she was still his little girl. She'd called to say she wouldn't be at the rest area. They'd gone to eat, and she'd see him at home. He didn't like the idea of the two of them out in public. He wasn't sure about them being alone together, either. Not yet.

He looked at his watch. *They'll probably beat me home, but not by much.* He was tempted to call her, but she was all grown up. He needed to treat her like an adult. He said a prayer for her and drove for home.

Arcon still made no mention of their eight years of communications—no chatting about the plans to get him out. Not even the rescue. Elaina bit her tongue. She'd wait until they were home.

Arcon noticed Elaina waved at everyone who drove a car like hers, and they'd wave back. He asked, "Do you know all those people?"

She laughed. "Of course not."

"Then why do they wave at you?"

"Because we drive the same car, a three-wheeled autocycle."

"What's an autocycle?"

"Remember when you rode in dad's car, you sat side-by-side and there was metal all around you?"

"Yes. It was better for talking."

"Uh, yeah. Well, in this one you sit behind me."

"This one is better for seeing."

"Yes, it is. Well, a vehicle where people sit one in front and one in back usually has two wheels and doesn't have metal around you. It's called a motorcycle."

"I've read about those."

"Well, this one is like halfway between those two. It has three wheels and is surrounded by metal, so they call it an autocycle. Wait, do you see that one coming toward us? See how it only has two wheels? That's a motorcycle."

Arcon looked closely as it passed by and said, "It looks like when children ride a goat. They hold on to its horns like that."

Elaina had to laugh, but she saw his point.

He was silent again for a few miles, then suddenly blurted out, "Messerschmitt."

"What did you just say?"

"I just remembered where I saw a vehicle like this. In the Room of Remembrance we have a book about unique autos. There was one like this with two wheels in the front and one in the back. It was called a Messerschmitt."

"Well, I'm glad they call this one a Tres."

"Did you say trace?"

"Yeah, like in uno, dos, tres. You know, because it has three wheels."

"Oh—okay. Spanish for three. I get it."

Most of the ride home was spent like that, with Arcon asking questions and offering unique observations. She enjoyed it a lot, but since the conversation never turned her direction, she was thankful when he fell asleep. One time he woke with a start and grabbed the back of her seat in a panic. Then he apologized and said he thought he was falling out of a tree.

"We're here," she said, when they arrived at the house. Her dad wasn't home yet, but she wasn't worried. He'd gone to meet with Ranger Dan and told her not to wait for him at the rest area.

She was looking forward to spending quiet time with Arcon and was glad he'd gotten some rest in the car. It had to have been a long day for him.

Of course, Arcon had questions. "Why did that light just come on?"

"It has a motion detector. It saw us and turned itself on."

"Without a generator?"

"The generator is a long ways away."

"You touched that button and another light came on. Ours did that."

"Another thing in common!"

"Do you have a toilet?"

"I was waiting for that one."

What she was really waiting for was to have a serious heart-to-heart discussion with him. Not about things, but about the two of them. She wanted to believe he'd risked everything to be with her. But even if that was temporary insanity—on her part or his—she needed to know where it went from here.

While Arcon was in the bathroom, she busied herself in the kitchen, making him some herbal tea with the hot tap. He'd talked at length about his grandma's herbal tea. It might be the best thing to help him be at ease until her dad arrived.

When she handed him the tea, she hoped he'd want to plop himself down in a comfortable chair. Instead, he continued marveling at his new surroundings. They both had running water, but hers ran faster. Her walls were smooth and colorful, theirs were logs. She decorated with pictures and paintings. Had she ever considered using car parts?

She laughed with him, and sometimes at him. He seemed to enjoy it all. She hoped his wonder at his new surroundings would eventually include her, but for the next ten minutes it did not. She finally tired of trying to stay in his line of sight and went to her favorite chair in the living room.

Roberto pulled into a parking spot to eat his hamburger. He'd realized he was hungry and probably wouldn't want to make a dinner once he got home. Before he started eating, he called Elaina to let her know he'd be getting there later.

He listened to it ringing and then got a recorded message. *Why wasn't she answering?* He decided to eat his meal and try her again.

The reporter had said she'd find out where he lived. He pictured a bunch of reporters outside his home trying to interview Arcon. He imagined them calling the authorities. It would make for better news if this escapee from the Mojave got arrested.

He worried Elaina would try to protect Arcon, and Arcon would try to protect her. The whole thing could get out of hand.

He shoved the last of the hamburger in his mouth and started the SRV. He hit autodial on his phone; still no answer. He waited a few seconds, tried again, and got the same results.

He spilled some of his coffee backing out too fast. He didn't care. He had to get home.

Arcon was about to remark on a picture of her and Roberto when he realized she was no longer in the room. He'd spent most of his life enthralled with discovering things. Other people helped him understand the world around him, but he always preferred to explore on his own. Now he was alone and didn't like it. He found Elaina sitting in the big room. "Would you like to be alone?"

"Absolutely not," she said.

"Good. Me neither," he said, sitting down on the sofa. He was glad she didn't wish to be alone, because he was longing to get to know her. But, at the moment, he had no clue how to start such a conversation. He was running out of small talk, but was doing his best.

He had no point of reference for carrying on a romantic conversation. "Can I ask you something?"

Her face brightened. "Of course."

"Can we do what you said at the ranger station?" He hoped she remembered as vividly as he did.

"Could you give me a clue?"

"Outside, before we went into the station." He gave her a moment to think about it, but she only looked confused. "Could you try to talk my ear off?"

Elaina laughed. "You don't know what you're asking for."

He was sure she'd meant it as a joke, but he was serious. Staring at the floor, he said, "In our community there are many people in a small space. As children, we're taught to listen more and talk less. But even with few talking there's too much to listen to. We go to our own homes to stop listening. Right now, I want to listen to you."

Elaina suddenly understood. She imagined him as a painter with a blank canvas and no paints. He had a vision with no way to express it. "How about a compromise?"

"What do you mean?"

"We both talk, and we both listen."

Arcon sighed. "I like that better."

"What shall we talk about first?"

"You," he said. "I don't know you. For years I've had you in my head. I talked to you there, and I talked to God about you."

He touched his ears. "Now we're in the same place together. But you're different."

Elaina felt a twinge of anxiousness. She was starting to give in to her insecurities. She was short; he was tall. She had a dark complexion, and he was fair. Some boys found her attractive, but most didn't seem impressed. She braced for rejection. "Are you disappointed?"

"Honestly, I am. Disappointed by my lack of imagination. I'm very pleased with what I see."

Elaina didn't know anyone who talked like Arcon, so direct. It embarrassed her, but in a pleasant way. She hung her head. "To be honest, I was afraid to get close to you at first." She gave him a coy look and a grin.

Arcon burst out laughing. "I must have looked so uncivilized."

"Don't take this wrong, but you actually looked like we expected, living in the forest and all."

"But I cleaned up okay, right?"

"I sure think so," she said, staring him up and down. "I can't wait to see you after a shower."

Arcon's eyes widened. Elaina realized her faux pas and quickly added, "With a set of clothes on that fit right."

He got to his feet and tugged on the baggy pant legs. "It does look kinda strange, doesn't it?"

Elaina stood as well. "But I like it."

He looked her in the eyes. "Do you like it enough to do what you did the first time you saw me wearing them?"

She did, but had to answer honestly, "Yes, but there's something between us."

His countenance dropped. With a furrowed brow he asked, "What is it?"

She held his stare for a moment. "The coffee table."

He glanced down. He smiled wide and took two steps to the side.

They walked toward each other, and she asked, "Does your arm still hurt?"

He held his arms open. "Not enough to stop me."

She threw her arms around him. "Then welcome to my world again, baggy pants."

The ice was broken. From this point on she could talk comfortably, and discover how different, and alike, they really were. And this time there was no one around to make her feel awkward about their embrace.

At twenty-one years old, Elaina had experienced a few relationships with boys, but nothing came close to what she felt at this moment. She didn't know for sure what was different. She didn't care. Her heart told her she wasn't letting go of him until she heard a car in the driveway. Maybe not until after the motion detector kicked on.

Arcon thought about the first time they'd met, on the west side of the Rift. The first time she'd touched him. He hadn't known how to respond, other than to be a total goofball.

Then he remembered how she'd hugged him at the ranger station. The Community hugged a lot, but it had never felt like that. Elaina's hug seemed to melt the anxiety out of him. Now it was happening again.

For the first time in a long while, he wasn't thinking about leaving. He'd arrived. This was the place he was meant to be.

He would take his time. Get to know Elaina and her dad. Learn how to fit into this society. He even thought he'd eventually give Roberto a Request for the Daughter's Hand—when the time was right. And, he didn't care if he ever saw the ArcPoint Forest again.

This had been one of the longest weeks in his life, and one of the most difficult, but tomorrow he could rest.

God had other plans.

AFTERWORD

These are certainly exciting times we're living in. But if you're the type of person who prefers less drama and a little more peace, let me introduce you to the people time forgot—but God remembered—in the land of ArcPoint.

Most stories about post-apocalyptic times focus on the destruction that took place, and the miserable conditions that resulted. Mojave Rift takes a Biblical viewpoint, and the hope that results when God is in control, literally.

The story takes place in the year 2165. The Biblical seven-year tribulation period transpired sometime in the first half of the 21st century. That era of conflict, lawlessness, and natural disasters ended when Jesus Christ returned. Since then, the world has enjoyed over a century of rebuilding from the devastation.

When Jesus *first* appeared, the Pharisees and other religious leaders failed to recognize Him because he didn't fit their perception of the Messiah. In the present day, as we approach Jesus' second coming, we need to ask ourselves, will it take place exactly like we expect? Could it come to pass differently? And then what happens?

Mojave Rift skips ahead to address that last question. It speculates on how planet Earth develops after Jesus returns. For more than a century under His guidance it has been popular to care for one another, and selfishness has not been celebrated. But one small group of people missed the party.

When conditions in the world turned ugly, about three hundred people banded together and asked God to hide them from society. He honored their request and they've been hiding ever since. They call themselves the ArcPoint Community Endeavor. Before we look at them, let's look at the world around them and how it came to be.

Based on over eight hundred Bible verses, this scenario of the future makes certain assumptions:

- It occurs during the thousand-year period mentioned in Revelation 20, and this particular period began when Jesus returned at the end of the seven-year tribulation era.

- It takes as literal that the earth was created in six days approximately six thousand years prior to the beginning of the 21st century, calculated on genealogy found in the gospels of Matthew and Luke, and the extra-biblical Book of Jubilees.

- It assumes the phrase "a day is as a thousand years" in 2 Peter 3:8 links the six-day creation with the six millennium age of the earth.

- Relative to this, the seventh day of creation—the day God rested—is linked to the thousand years in Revelation 20 and is referred to by Paul in Hebrews 4:9 as a Sabbath rest for mankind, due to the removal of evil that had afflicted the earth for six thousand years.

- It assumes Jesus is the Lord referred to in Isaiah 2:2-4 and Jeremiah 3:14-18. It also assumes Zion and Jerusalem referenced in these verses are physically located in the land of Israel.

- Isaiah 9:6, the well-known verse describing the Messiah states, "… the Government will rest on His shoulders." This is the case in Mojave Rift, where successive levels of authority handle governance of the earth with Jesus as the ultimate authority.

- With the Man of Lawlessness revealed and defeated, respect for the law is restored to mankind. However, Isaiah 2:4 says, "… He shall judge among the nations, and shall rebuke many people." This indicates a form of judicial system may still be necessary, and so judges are used as arbiters.

- Finances are earned and shared, rather than stolen or hoarded (Ephesians 4:28).

- Lifespans are longer, for a variety of reasons. Life expectancy increases to beyond a hundred years old, with many living as long as Abraham, Isaac, and Jacob.

- Due to many Bible references about God supplying or withholding rain, in the future He alters climate patterns to ensure more areas of the planet will support agriculture. Especially the Mojave Desert.

Now let's examine the plight of the ArcPoint people themselves. In the beginning, they were simply reacting to the rise in crime around them. When an opportunity to hide presented itself, they took advantage. But soon, evil reared its ugly head within ArcPoint itself.

On the verge of collapse, they asked God to remove evil from their midst and never let it return. Such was His plan for all of mankind, but it wouldn't take place until the world experienced seven years of unrestrained evil. ArcPoint received that gift a few years earlier than the rest of mankind.

As with Noah, Abraham, and Moses, God separated the ArcPoint people unto Himself. Although His people had a history of regressing back to their evil ways, when the ArcPoint people asked for that separation—unanimously and sincerely—he complied.

Due to natural forces of an aging planet, a major tectonic event was about to shake Southern California. God aligned the event to happen away from the most populous areas, and create a barrier for the ArcPoint people. The land pulled apart, creating a series of canyons that stretched nearly four hundred miles from southern California to northern Nevada. It was officially named The CalNeva Rift. Two interstate highways, the I-15 to Nevada and the I-40 to Arizona, became impassable.

Soon after, Jesus returned. He removed the evil spirits that had afflicted humans since Adam's time, binding them from returning to the physical world. For a thousand years mankind would be free from that form of spiritual temptation and conflict.

With no one traveling through their area, the ArcPoint people enjoyed peace and security. Every year they would vote on whether to rejoin the rest of the world, or continue to trust God on their own. Over the years they renewed their request annually for God to keep them separated unto Himself. Jesus made it official when he established the Mojave Restricted Area as a sanctuary for the Mojave People.

There's not much drama in the ArcPoint Community. The only member who was uncomfortable with that was Arcon Franklin. A cage-rattler. But he's gone now, and life has returned to the status quo. It will, until the return of Arcon—the MOJAVE MAN.

J.W. GILBERT

MOJAVE
MAN

Read on for a sneak peek at the next ArcPoint
book from JW Gilbert Books.

MOJAVE MAN

BOOK 2 *of the* ARCPOINT SERIES

CHAPTER ONE

Roberto shoved the last chicken nugget in his mouth and moved the Search and Rescue Vehicle into the right lane. His Personal Information Device was repeating a series of tones that identified the messenger as Ranger Dan. Roberto pulled into a grocery store parking lot and grabbed the first spot he saw. He reset the PID and opened his comm-pad. The message read: HIDE TARZAN NOW. KEEP IN TOUCH. SECURE. *Great. What could have happened?*

He tapped a button on the steering wheel and said, "Call Elaina." He put away the comm-pad and listened to the phone ring on the car speakers. *Come on, girl, where are you? You always have your phone with you.*

He put the SRV in gear, snaked through the lot, and darted back into traffic. There were only a few miles to go, but cross traffic seemed to steal the right of way at every intersection. *Can't catch a break.* At the next yellow light, he stepped on the gas, seeing it turn red just as he passed under it. *Be patient. You don't want any company right now.*

If this was an official concern, he could call in for favored traffic flow or turn on his lights and sirens. *But what would I say? I need help to avoid the authorities?* He slowed the SRV down some, but his mind was still racing. One dangerous scenario after another filled his thoughts.

Could that reporter have found their home address that fast? Would she have called the authorities on her own regarding Arcon? What would Arcon do if a crowd suddenly descended on him? What if he thought someone was threatening Elaina? Roberto hit the redial button. No response. *What if they never made it home?*

He was about to hit redial once more when he heard another tone from the PID. It was Ranger Dan again. He wheeled to the side of the road and opened his comm-pad. Have Location 4U. South. 447YB811V.

Roberto breathed a sigh of relief. Ranger Dan must have located a place to hide Arcon. At this point, he had no other choice than to trust the Ranger. Roberto got back on the road, mashed the pedal to the floor, and prayed he wasn't too late.

Elaina melted into Arcon's firm embrace. She'd need to explain so much to him, especially how he was a fugitive in this world. Later. This moment, this touch, had been a long time coming. She'd feared it never would. Now there were even more things to be afraid of. Ranger Dan ought never to have allowed her dad to have custody of this escapee from the Mojave Forest.

The law stated: 'Anything coming from that location must be quarantined until proper judgment can be made by the authorities having jurisdiction for both that area and the locality where that entity may be relocated.' Her dad had pounded that rule into her, then surprised her by breaking it himself. *This house doesn't qualify for quarantine. Ranger Dan isn't the authority over this area. What were those two thinking? Neither of them are Judges.*

Elaina believed that, in the eyes of the Authorities, Arcon would be considered innocent. He was a good, kind, honest man. Now that he wasn't running around dressed like Tarzan, they'd be sure to see him as more than just a Mojave man. Everyone would come to understand—Arcon isn't a leper.

Elaina knew no one really believed people in the protected area were diseased. But that's how many people viewed the Mojave Restricted Area—like the leper colonies of the Middle Ages. Only it wasn't a physical disease. It was like some form of spiritual leprosy. *Pity those poor people, but don't go near them.* When that thought came to her, she just hugged Arcon harder. Any quarantine he'd have to face, she would endure with him. Her greatest fear was they'd send him back to the Mojave.

Arcon's immediate future was a mystery, but hers was not. She knew the moment they heard her dad's car in the driveway, this embrace would end, followed shortly thereafter by a lecture from her dad. She'd forgotten her shoulder-phone in the car and was long overdue to check in with him. But she refused to stop what she was doing to retrieve it.

After the drama of getting Arcon across the Rift, she'd hoped for a few days of tranquility, a chance to be with Arcon before they turned him over to the Authorities. They'd isolate him in a secure location. He'd be questioned, probed, tested, and watched, trading his prison in the Mojave for another in this world. It was important she had time to prepare him.

Maybe her dad was right. She should never have encouraged him to leave his people. But she firmly believed Arcon would be a free man someday. She just needed to explain the procedure so he could endure the trial. But she wasn't about to end their embrace for that either.

Ranger Dan paced outside the station, waiting for Roberto and refusing to take any more calls. The reporter for the San Bernardino Portal was not satisfied with his 'no comment at this time.' routine. *She won't rest until she finds out who rescued Arcon. This human-interest story will morph into a manhunt and an inquiry.*

Then the news will hit the surrounding states, and those with Calneva Rift alerts on their searchnet device. He walked across the parking lot and stared at the broad expanse of the Rift.

Why had I been in such a hurry? He'd been prepared—and excited—about the prospect of meeting the Mojave People someday. He'd studied the laws regarding the containment procedure. The population would be quarantined, given physical and psychological exams, and treated fairly. Had he stuck to protocol, the original plan would have let the Authorities judge Arcon, and his fate would've been determined. Then various localities would've sponsored him with a home, job, and—most importantly—supervision.

But Dan hadn't followed the rules. Instead, he'd gotten caught up in the novelty of giving freedom to a naïve, polite, young Mojave man clad in animal skins. Dan had let his own curiosity and excitement get the better of him. The only way to make things right was to recapture Arcon. Dan's plan revolved around the two people who'd assisted Arcon to leave that area. If he could control the actions of Roberto and Elaina, he'd be able to contain Arcon and make things right.

But now Dan had a reporter dogging him. All he could hope for was to get Arcon hidden away before she took the story public. If suddenly confronted with the unknown, any man's instinct is to fight or take flight. Whether a bee or a bear, the panic is genuine. If Arcon felt threatened by an onslaught of news crews, his reaction could be perilous.

At the moment, Dan despised the Mojave Restricted Area even more than usual. The hassles of dealing with those who obsessed about the Mojave People frequently eclipsed his duties as Park Ranger. Anyone, from the casual tourist, clear up to the Peace Regulators that governed human interaction, was biased and afraid of what may lie beyond the Rift. It didn't help that it had once been a desert area called *Devil's Playground*.

As Chief of the Calneva Rift Ranger station, all Rift related inquiries funneled through him. As Authority over the Mojave Forest, they expected him to be in control of what happened around the Restricted Area. The higher authorities allowed only a 24-hour window to locate and confine Arcon to a safe location. After that, they would activate the Open Eyes protocol.

Ranger Becca was already gathering video footage for the search algorithms. Stills from the Ranger station cameras of Arcon in his Tarzan suit, his new apparel, even the scars on his arms, were all to be cataloged. So were pictures of Roberto, Elaina, and their vehicles. Becca had already logged the Gonzales' employment with San Bernardino Search and Rescue, as well as their home address.

Ranger Dan glanced at his watch. He had a meeting at 10AM on Monday with Sir Nelson, the Authority over Southern California. *I'll request the Open Eyes protocol be postponed until after that meeting.* He knew if Arcon wasn't in a secure location by then, he'd need to be found fast. With a tap on a keyboard, the protocol would activate thousands of surveillance cameras in a radius of five hundred miles. If the cameras spotted any of the images Becca just input, the Rangers would receive an alert.

Dan at least needed to know if Arcon was still with the rescuers. *Why aren't they contacting me? What if they're avoiding the cameras?* He started pacing again as he waited for a response.

ORDER MOJAVE MAN TODAY!

JWGILBERTBOOKS.COM

JOHN WOZNIAK IS A CHRISTIAN FICTION WRITER with a knack for stories, research, and rock hunting. He and his wife are life-long Oregon residents with a passion for discovering the beauty in rocks and the One who created them. John's goal is to create rather than destroy, conserve rather than waste, hope rather than despair, and to laugh rather than weep. These goals have served him well, even when he was determined to remain an atheist.

Life altering experiences drove John to write his second book: Escaping Ignorance—Pursuing Wisdom: More Than 150 Stories Revealing God's Grace, Guidance, and Goodness in the Life of a Former Atheist. He's been writing ever since, honing his skills, and making headway with editing and self-publishing.

Before retiring, John worked as an international trouble-shooter for data-center cooling. He now draws readily from his years in research to shape realistic environments for his characters. Mojave Rift, the award-winning first book in his post-apocalyptic series, takes place many decades from now in the once desert regions of California. John has spent thousands of hours researching science trends and comparing them to Bible prophecy for this series. *"I've sought expert advice in computers, energy, climatology, genetics, botany, geology, transportation, and other fields."*

John is also having a lot of fun creating characters who are admirable without being super-human. He writes characters who lend a helping hand rather than a swift kick. He's met those kinds of people, and tries hard to emulate them. Many of their positive traits are portrayed in the characters of John's books. *"In the Bible, I discovered predictions for a time when these attitudes would be normal, without being forced. My desire is for the reader to discover the same hope I did."*

For more about JW and the saga of Arcon, please visit:

JWGILBERTBOOKS.COM